MISADVENTURES WITH A SEXPERT

MISADVENTURES WITH A SEXPERT

BY
ELIZABETH HAYLEY

This book is an original publication of Waterhouse Press.

Cover Design by Waterhouse Press
Cover Images: Shutterstock

ISBN: 978-1-64263-203-3

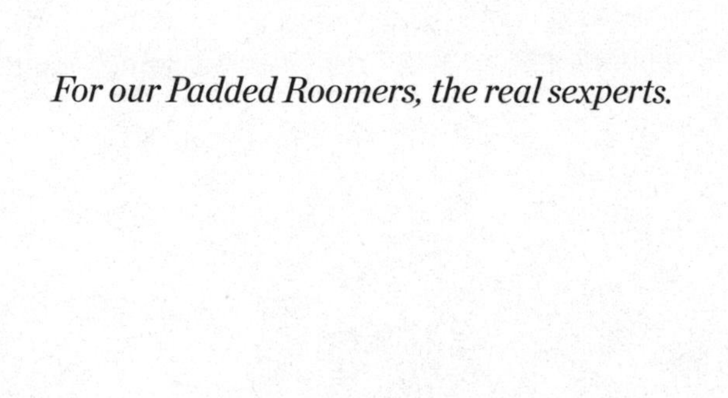

For our Padded Roomers, the real sexperts.

CHAPTER ONE

GRAYSON

"Yo, Grayson. Boss Man wants to see you."

As I sat behind my desk, looking through pictures I'd taken this morning of an elderly women's knitting circle, I willed myself to take deep breaths. If I'd known ten years ago I would one day be beckoned by a stoner serving as the intercom for my disheveled and squirrelly "boss man," Mr. Thomas, I would have quickly sought out the nearest set of knitting needles and jabbed them into my ears.

Instead, I slowly rose, turned, and waved to Dax—our resident intercom extraordinaire and film critic who only watched horror movies—before making my way to what Mr. Thomas considered his office.

It was, in fact, more of a closet, with a small desk that must have been assembled inside it because there was no way it would have fit through the doorway. There were also two small filing cabinets stacked one on top of the other, a metal stationary chair for Mr. Thomas, and a stool for whomever he dragged inside.

"You wanted to see me, sir?"

"Ah, yes, Hawk, come on in. Close the door behind you."

"It's Hawkins, sir."

"What?" The man's beady eyes shrank even more,

making his confusion clear.

"My last name. It's Hawkins, not Hawk. You could just call me Grayson, or Gray, if you'd like."

"If I wanted to call you a color, I already would have. A hawk is highly intelligent and has exceptional eyesight. Can the same be said of you?"

Accepting the battle was already lost, I shook my head.

"I didn't think so. You should be flattered to be compared to a bird of that caliber."

"I wasn't thinking of it that way," I muttered as I accepted defeat.

To close the door, I had to crowd his desk, nearly toppling over the stool as I wedged my way in. Once that ordeal was over, I righted my seat, sat, and propped my foot on one of the rungs of the stool.

He leaned forward, rested his elbows on his desk, and steepled his fingers. "I've let Willow go."

The sole of my shoe slipped off the stool's rung, causing me to lurch forward and almost careen into the desk.

"Oh. That's a shame," I said as I sat back down.

I found myself secretly envying Willow, the person in charge of maintaining our social media accounts. Or who used to, anyway. I wasn't exactly sure what it took to get fired from the *Daily Gazette*, but I was hoping to find out. The story behind it would probably be the most newsworthy thing to enter the office in quite some time.

Though as I had that thought, I also realized I wasn't being fair. I didn't *have* to be here. Every day, instead of saying "fuck this place" like a normal functioning adult would, I came into this looney bin of a newspaper office.

It was supposed to be a way for me to find myself again

in a low-pressure environment after leaving the opposite in New York, but the place had more loonies than a subway car after last call.

"Hmm, yes, it is a shame. For her. She's not getting a reference from me, that's for sure."

"What did she do?" I asked.

He waved me off. "You know I'm not one to spread rumors." Which was a bald-faced lie. The man would've made the editors at the *National Enquirer* salivate with the way he traded gossip. "But let me warn you that putting your own personal ads into our paper won't be tolerated. I still don't even know what *D slash s* means, and part of me hopes I never find out."

Nodding along like the good plebeian I was, I tried to figure out what any of this had to do with me.

"Anyway," he continued, "I'll need you to take over her job for the foreseeable future." He began moving papers around on his desk as if the conversation was over. Which it wasn't. Not by a long shot.

"I'm sorry, what now?"

"Well, I figured since you already take all our pictures, you could just upload them to our social media accounts, add a few pithy comments, and voilà, you're done."

"But . . . I hate social media. I don't even have a Facebook page of my own."

"I'm sure you'll make it work. Willow did it. How hard can it be?"

"I thought you were considering letting me draw some comics for the paper. Social media coordinator is a far cry from that."

When I'd moved to town and interviewed for the

photographer's job at the *Daily Gazette,* I'd expressed my true goal was to *create* pictures instead of just snapping photographs. Being a photojournalist had been lucrative for me, but I wanted . . . more. And my early midlife crisis was as good a time as any to make that happen.

Mr. Thomas had told me that while the paper didn't currently have a comic section, he wasn't opposed to the idea. Though six months later, I still hadn't been given the green light to draw anything.

"Hawkins, we don't *need* comics for a paper. We do need subscribers to buy said paper, though. And creating a presence on social media is a big part of accomplishing that."

He must have realized I was about to tell him to shove this job down his smarmy throat, because he quickly sat back and looked at me intently.

"Tell you what. You can work some of your comics into your social media posts. If they attract attention, I'll let you start adding them to the paper. How about that?" His face looked like an eager Cocker Spaniel's, and that was probably the only thing that kept me from smacking him.

I wanted to rail against this man and this insignificant job, but I didn't. I'd gained a good deal of notoriety for my photos over the years and had even been featured in *National Geographic* once. I'd traveled the world and met interesting people, but none of it meant anything because it wasn't what I wanted. It hadn't made me who I'd truly wanted to be when I was a kid devouring comic books for inspiration.

So instead of telling Mr. Thomas to shove this social media bullshit up his ass, I found myself saying, "Do you have a list of the accounts and passwords?"

CHAPTER TWO

GRAYSON

"Eff my life," I whispered for at least the twentieth time in two hours. That was how long I'd been sitting in the Coffee Bean, the local coffee shop I'd started to frequent just to get out of the house. It was also how long I'd been tinkering with some of my most recent photos—a task that wasn't nearly as thrilling as taking them.

It was just about the only thing I missed about my old job. Someone else edited the photos so I didn't have to. As I clicked on various buttons to brighten up the background or adjust contrast, my fingers itched to draw.

Ever since I'd moved to Monroe six months ago, I'd been coming to the Bean a few nights a week, and I'd hoped that being out in public and surrounded by people would get my creative juices flowing. Now that I had Mr. Thomas's permission to post some of my drawings on Instagram, I was more eager than ever to create something the public would find as interesting as I did. Unfortunately, I hadn't found anything yet.

Not that the people I observed at the coffee shop weren't interesting. Tonight I had the pleasure of observing an elderly woman who wore a magenta mink coat despite it being a mild spring day. She kept darting her eyes around the room before dropping pieces of her muffin into her purse. I hoped like hell she had a pet in there she was feeding.

Then there was the middle-aged man dressed in a business suit sitting by the window, talking loudly on his cell phone in between voracious bites of a croissant sandwich. He kept saying things like “live a little” and “how do you *know* you wouldn’t like it?” My mind ran through a variety of possibilities for what they could be talking about. Rock climbing? Skydiving? Bondage? Pegging? The options were endless.

A young blond-haired guy was typing frantically at another table. I wanted to storm over there and demand to know what he was writing about. How dare he have direction and inspiration while I sat here slurping tepid coffee and cursing whichever muse was in charge of creative thinkers? Because that bitch had fallen asleep on the job.

If I were being truthful, she’d left way before I’d left New York and its mile-a-minute pace I had to abandon once my life became a living joke—with me as the punch line. Too bad no one found it funny.

Or maybe they might. Maybe I should draw up a visual of my last few months, because who wouldn’t want to laugh about a train wreck of a marriage? That was one thing I’d learned from my years as a photojournalist: human beings loved depressing shit. As long as it wasn’t their *own* shit.

It might make them feel better about the poor grades they’d earned in grad school or the credit card they couldn’t pay off because they’d spent their money on courtside Knicks tickets. At least they could be thankful their wife wasn’t banging their best friend.

Scrubbing my hands over my face, I groaned quietly.

To hell with it. With my editing done and nothing worth drawing, I would just have to try again tomorrow night.

Just as I was about to close my laptop, the bell above the door jingled, signaling a new customer. I glanced up as I began to lower the lid, but I halted the motion. A woman with long black hair entered and approached the counter. I opened the laptop again so I could pretend to work while I watched her order.

She smiled at the barista and ordered something I couldn't make out, and then she paid and waited patiently for her drink. I was more than happy when she took a seat two tables away, facing me. She offered me a small smile, and I averted my gaze, realizing I'd been staring.

I wasn't quite sure what it was about her, but I was drawn to her—though certainly not in a way that established any sort of romantic interest. That ship had sailed... before hitting an iceberg in the middle of the Atlantic and sinking to the depths of the ocean, never to be seen again. My heart would *not* go on. But I could still find someone attractive, sexually speaking. I was a red-blooded male, after all.

The woman's dark hair was bone straight and glistened like she starred in Pantene commercials. Wearing tight black jeans and some kind of white gauzy top that was off her shoulders, my attention was drawn to her collarbones, which I never realized I was into before now, but it was a revelation.

I also realized I was skirting the same level of creeper status as the guy in the business suit, but I no longer felt like leaving, so I attempted to refocus.

A few minutes later, the bell sounded again, and a guy walked in wearing a polo that was stretched so tightly over his protruding muscles, I thought one wrong move might cause the entire thing to shred into tatters. He didn't approach the counter but instead scanned the room and began walking toward the raven-haired woman.

"Hey. You Elsa?" the guy asked, his voice gruff.

The woman stood and stretched a hand toward the brute. "Isla actually. Long *I*, and the *S* is silent. Nice to meet you. Mick, right?"

"Yeah, that's me. Sorry I'm a little late. I got held up at the gym."

Of course you did, I thought as I watched Muscles McGee sit down.

To keep my eyes off the man and look busy, I clicked around aimlessly on the internet. But before I knew it, I was doodling in my notebook—bulging biceps and veins, an exaggerated forehead, and a jaw so square, a geometry teacher could use it to teach right angles.

I used to sketch constantly in high school, but that was before I got married to Miranda and got caught up in the rat race that was New York City. I hadn't been drawing as much as I'd have liked over the past few years, but I was trying to fix that now.

It made me wonder why I hadn't drawn any caricatures of Dennis sticking his dick in my wife on the granite countertop of the kitchen I paid for.

"No worries," the woman—Isla—said as she also lowered to her seat.

The two sat in silence that made even me feel awkward. Then Isla said, "So, tell me about yourself."

I looked up from my sketchbook and typed nonsense on the keyboard so I could focus on the man's reply, but the gods weren't on my side. A couple walked in, and the six or so employees of the coffee shop all squealed.

A loud, "Hey, bitches," pierced through the air as a short, well-endowed woman struck a pose. "Did Jamaica agree with me or what?" They all started asking questions about what had evidently been the couple's honeymoon.

None of them seemed to care that they were turning the quiet shop into a noisy hub. Unable to make out the finer points of the conversation between Isla and Mick, I went back to my visual representation.

The couple went behind the counter, making me think they also worked here, as their decibel level ebbed and flowed like ocean waves.

In between outbursts, I was able to learn that Mick was training to be an MMA fighter, but his coach was currently in prison on some "bullshit charges," so he was working as a trainer in the meantime. He was also Instagram famous and was contemplating starting an OnlyFans. I didn't exactly know what that meant and wasn't sure how this guy would be capable of getting "fans," but that made it even more impressive. Maybe I should ask for some pointers.

I couldn't hear what Isla did for a living, but I did make out that she hadn't dated in a while, went to the gym sporadically, and was interested in monogamy. It might have been my imagination, but I thought she'd stressed the word *monogamy* on purpose. If she had, I hoped it had the desired effect, because Mick couldn't quite keep the disgust off his face and didn't stay much longer.

The couple that had returned from Jamaica didn't stay much longer than Mick, the woman claiming she'd see them in the "salt mines" tomorrow. With their departure, all was quiet again, which I was grateful for as Isla grabbed her cell phone and made a call.

"Hey." She sighed heavily. "I should've listened to you. He was as horrible as you predicted." Isla smiled as she listened to whoever was on the other end of the line. "I had to go out with him. He was the only one who messaged me who could actually meet up this week." She listened again for a moment before continuing. "You and Kaitlynn are the ones who made me promise to go on one date a week. I'm only holding up my end of the bargain."

Now I was even more curious than I *had* been. Was she doing some kind of dating experiment? Was she actually interested in any of these guys, or was she just getting her rocks off by leading them on?

"You should've seen it. I mentioned monogamy, and he practically flew out of here," Isla continued. "I made a new profile on a different app and have a couple of messages that look more promising. I think I'm going to stick to Wednesday nights at the Coffee Bean. That way, if I go missing, you have a starting point to begin the search."

I heard a screech through the phone.

Isla laughed. "No, I don't think that's funny. I'm sorry my hypothetical kidnapping upset you. Okay. Got it. Yes. I'll call you tomorrow. I'll tell her. I promise. Bye."

Chuckling, Isla placed her phone on the table and rummaged around in her large purse, pulling a tablet from it. She cast a glance my way, making me avert my eyes quickly again so I didn't appear like the stalker I was kind of guilty of being.

As she began typing away on her tablet and sipping her coffee, I thought about leaving, but something stopped me. It was like my muse had finally woken the fuck up and was poking at my brain with an idea I couldn't quite latch on to yet.

Sometime later the bell over the door jingled, but I didn't look up to see who entered. Not until a deep voice said, "Are you Isla?" did I raise my head. Had she been perusing her hookup apps on her tablet this whole time? Jesus, this chick was savage.

"Um, yes. Do I know you?" she asked, sounding truly confused.

My eyes were glued to my laptop screen, but my ears were hanging on every word of their exchange.

"It's me. Patrick."

"I'm sorry"—and I had to give her credit because she actually did sound sorry—"but I don't think we've met."

"Yeah, I know. That's why I'm here. To meet."

I couldn't resist. I sneaked a glance at them and saw a tall, thin man with a genuine smile looking down at Isla, whose face was scrunched up like she'd sucked on a lemon.

"Have you ever known exactly where you were but still been lost?" she asked.

I snorted, causing both of them to look my way. I tried to cover it with a cough, but I was sure it was an unsuccessful diversion.

"I'm not sure what you mean," Patrick replied.

"Never mind. So how do we know each other?"

"We don't."

"That's . . . unhelpfully vague."

Patrick began to reply but was interrupted by another man I hadn't even heard come in. "Hi. You must be Isla. I'm Chase."

Then I gave up all pretense and began openly staring at the spectacle in front of me. Chase was smaller and more compact than Patrick, but their fair complexions were strikingly similar.

"Hi, Chase," Isla said, her words wary. "May I ask, why must I be Isla?"

"Are you?" he asked.

"Well, yes, but—"

"Then that's why you have to be." Chase looked proud of his deduction, which made him endearing. Sort of like a three-legged puppy with a permanently lolling tongue.

"Let me rephrase," Isla said. "How do you know my name?"

"Your profile said it."

"What profile?"

"Your dating profile." Chase looked over at Patrick, seemingly concerned that Isla clearly had no idea who he was. "Hey, man. What's up?" Chase extended a hand, which Patrick took after a beat and muttered his name. Then Chase pointed between the two of them. "Is this like a threesome thing? Because I've never done that, but I could probably get into it."

Patrick jerked his head back a little at that, but once he recovered, he looked at Isla with an expression that could only be described as hopeful.

Isla stood then and put her hands out in front of her. "Let's back up about a million steps. How did you know from my dating profile that I'd be here?"

"Because you messaged me and told me to meet you here. I know I'm early, but I was in the neighborhood."

Isla's brow furrowed. "That doesn't make any… Oh for fuck's sake, Olivia."

Both men whirled around as if to look for someone named Olivia popping up behind them. They then slowly panned back toward her as if they'd just been informed she'd recently escaped from Arkham Asylum.

"Sorry. That's my sister. I talked to her earlier and . . . that doesn't matter. Anyway, she created my profile, and I never changed the password. It was probably she who messaged you because she's a meddling brat. It's the only thing that seems plausible. I'm so sorry."

Both men looked baffled, like she'd spoken to them in Arabic.

"So is Olivia coming or . . . ?" Patrick asked.

It was Isla's turn to look like she was speaking to a moron. "No. She made the dates with you on my behalf. But she didn't bother telling *me* about it, so I wasn't expecting you."

"Does that mean a threesome is on or off the table?" Chase asked, God bless him.

"It's off the table. Like, far off," Isla replied.

"Bummer." Chase pushed his hands into the pockets of his well-worn jeans and looked at Patrick. "So where do we go from here?"

"I think we all go home," Isla supplied. Chase's face perked up, so she hurriedly added, "To our own homes. Alone."

He deflated again and rocked on his heels.

Patrick took that as his cue to speak up. "Can we set up another time to get together with you?"

My ears caught on the use of "we," and it seemed Isla's did too.

"I don't think that's a good idea," she said.

Patrick shrugged and turned to Chase. "There's a bar down the block. Want to go try our luck there?"

Chase's smile was so wide, it nearly spanned the entire lower half of his face. "Hell yeah."

Patrick smiled at his new best threesome buddy, and

after both of them said quick goodbyes to Isla, they took off for the door.

Isla continued to stand as she stared after them. “That was the weirdest experience of my entire life.”

I thought she meant it to be to herself, so I didn’t respond. I pretended to type as she gathered her things and headed for the door, only making a slight detour to throw away her cup.

I watched her leave, intrigued by what else Isla might be up to in the coming weeks. One thing was for certain. I was sure as hell going to be at the coffee shop next Wednesday.

CHAPTER THREE

GRAYSON

"Hawkins."

I spun in my swivel chair, thinking he'd at least used my complete last name this time, though the fact that he never called anyone by their first names made me wonder if he was doing it intentionally as a way of indirectly stripping us of our identities. Or maybe he was just bitter that his first name sounded like a last name and vice versa.

I expected to see Ellis Thomas stretching his tiny body to the corners of his office door as he yelled at me from across the room. He did this kind of thing often—putting himself into abnormal and sometimes unprofessional poses in an attempt to appear larger than the speck of a man he was. He stood at least a foot shorter than my six-four frame, and the suits he wore made him look like a toddler sporting his older brother's hand-me-downs before they fully fit him.

The last few weeks, Mr. Thomas had taken a liking to sitting on employees' desks and hovering above them awkwardly while he grilled them about their current projects or rambled about how the internet is to blame for the paper's steady decline in readers. When I saw the man coming toward my desk, I prayed his ass didn't end up on top of the area I'd recently Clorox-wiped for that exact reason.

"Did you get the email I sent?"

"What email are you referring to?" The guy sent more emails than a spammer, and most of them were even less relevant. Someone needed to tell him that no one had a cure for his dog's allergy to Greek yogurt, but that would involve replying, and no one was ever willing to do that.

"The email I just sent," he said with a shake of his head. And then to the room, "Aren't you Millennials like glued to electronic devices? Maybe if you'd stop Snapchatting pictures of your lunch, you'd get a little more work done."

"What's a Millennial?" Curtis whispered to someone I couldn't see from my vantage point. Curtis was about as old as the building itself, which to my knowledge used to serve as the town's first school.

"I think it's an energy drink," someone said.

"Ah, there's the email," I said as I scanned it. "You literally sent it a minute and a half ago."

My boss scoffed. "What's your point, Hawk?"

There it was again. "Never mind. It's not important."

Mr. Thomas stared at me for a few moments. "Well, are you going to show him around, or not?"

"Show who around?" Lynda asked. She'd just come in, large coffee in one hand and a Danish in the other, even though work had started almost an hour ago.

"Well, what do you know?" said Jessica. "Only an hour late today."

"Shut up, Jessicunt. I have glass coming out of my skin," she said.

I winced at the insult, but Jessica didn't even seem fazed by it. Though truthfully, my reaction should have been the unexpected one. I should be used to Lynda's mouth by now.

She released her large bag from her shoulder, letting it flop to the ground in a large heap that resembled a baby leopard that had fallen asleep on the faded gray carpet.

"I broke a glass the other day," Lynda explained, "and when I went to vacuum it up, I sneezed." Lynda dropped her body into her chair with the same gravitational pull that had worked on the bag. "I must've breathed in some of it, and now it's coming out through the skin on my arms."

"That's crazy," Jess said, placating her. She at least knew better than to rile her up more. Also, "that's crazy" was our code for "*you're* crazy" without actually saying it to Lynda's face.

"Are you finished oversharing?" Mr. Thomas shouted. "A journalism professor who wants to see if our paper's suitable for future internships is stopping by, and I need to know who's going to give him a tour."

"Is he hot?" Jess asked. "I can show him around."

"I'd be happy to take the professor around," I said, causing Jess to huff.

"I'm so tired of this sexist, male-dominated bullshit," she said. "It's like if you don't have a penis, you don't get to do anything important."

Lynda rolled her eyes. "Oh, calm down, Eleanor Roosevelt. I'll let you know when it's time to burn your bra."

Jess stuck her pierced tongue out at Lynda. "Like you'd know. You don't even own one."

"Ladies, ladies," Mr. Thomas said. "I don't care who takes the professor around as long as you don't mention your bras or the foreign substances working their way out of your bodies"—he shot a look toward Dax—"or into them. Figure it out. Just let me know what you decide."

He began walking toward his office but looked back at me as the women were bickering. *Make sure it's you,* he mouthed as he pointed a finger at me.

When Jess suggested we arm wrestle to decide who'd take the professor out, I seriously considered asking my coworkers to give me permission to post weekly comics about them on the paper's Instagram account. This place was a gold mine of material. An insufferable gold mine, but a gold mine nonetheless.

CHAPTER FOUR

ISLA

With a heavy sigh, I looked at the decor in the Bean like I hadn't been here a million times before. Worn brick, mahogany shelves showcasing merchandise, bar stools at a counter facing the street, and wooden floors that were made to appear rustic when I knew for a fact they'd been put in less than a year ago.

I used to come at least twice a week on my way to the office, and sometimes Thursday for a few hours if I was working from home. But ever since my pact with my sister, Olivia, I'd added Wednesday nights to the schedule. At first, I thought meeting my dates at a place I was comfortable with might lessen the awkwardness, but that didn't prove true.

Two of my favorite baristas had eventually realized I'd basically been running a dating service out of the place. They'd tossed their share of sarcastic jokes my way, but ultimately they made my experiences a little more interesting because I had someone to talk to about them afterward.

I'd been waiting about fifteen minutes when Blake came over with a fresh chamomile tea. "Is there some kind of rule like they have at college, where you get to leave if he doesn't show up after a certain amount of time?" She cleared my empty mug and set down the new one.

"I wish. Unfortunately, Professor Punctual already texted to see if I could wait a little longer. He forgot to get gas earlier, and he was running on E."

Blake shook her head. Somehow she managed to convey a sense of empathy despite her laugh. "I once dated a guy who went everywhere by skateboard. Be thankful he *has* a car." She gave me a wink before heading back behind the counter to help another customer.

A few minutes later, I was still thinking about how ridiculous it would be if Luca showed up on a skateboard, his hand extended and an apologetic smile spread across his surprisingly handsome face.

But I'd learned the hard way to be leery of pictures people posted on their profiles. It was evidently proper dating-app etiquette to choose a picture that looked nothing like the real thing.

"Isla? It's so nice to meet you. I'm sorry I'm late." After letting go of my hand, he pointed to the empty chair across from me. "May I sit?"

"Yes. Of course. Please."

We looked at each other for a few moments before he spoke. "Sorry if I'm staring," he said. "It's just that you're even more beautiful in person than you are in your pictures."

That made me smile, and I felt the comment draw some heat to my cheeks, no doubt bringing color to my usually pale skin.

"Thank you. I was thinking the same." It was probably the first time any of the men looked better in person than they did in their profile pictures. His short blond hair was a bit longer now, revealing some cute curls in the back, and he definitely didn't skip chest day at the gym.

He looked at me a little longer before I asked if he wanted to get something to drink before we talked.

He nodded. "Sure, I'll grab something. Can I get you anything?"

"No thanks," I said. And while he waited in line, I took a second to text my sister that Luca had just shown up, he was hot, and so far, seemed like a gentleman. Olivia made me promise to call as soon as I left.

When Luca returned with his coffee and a cheese Danish, I found myself feeling more excited for this date than I had about any of the others before it. He worked about two miles from the coffee shop as an investment advisor. "I've been with Millennium for a little over two years," he said. "It's been great so far. I can bring my dog to work."

"Seriously? I love dogs. What kind do you have?"

"A labradoodle named Chelsea."

I found myself leaning in a little as Luca talked, almost entranced by his clear blue eyes and the way his crisp button-down fit perfectly across his chest and shoulders. The man definitely worked out. Though thankfully not as much as Mick.

"Chelsea's a cute name for a dog. Where'd you come up with it?"

"Oh, I can't take credit for that. My girlfriend named her. She went to college in New York."

My eyes widened as I struggled to swallow the sip of tea I'd just taken. "I'm assuming you mean your *ex*-girlfriend?"

Luca looked genuinely confused. "No, Marybeth and I live together."

"You live together!"

"Oh, yeah, sorry. Is that a problem? Because it's not for

Marybeth. She's cool with it."

"She's cool with you having online dating profiles and seeing other women?"

"Yeah. Or men. We identify as relationship queer." He sat back in his chair with an air of superiority. Like he and... Marybeth were somehow more progressive than me and my antiquated monogamist ideals.

"That's not even a real term." I would've laughed if my current situation wasn't so sad.

Luca rolled his unfortunately gorgeous blue eyes. "That's exactly what someone who adheres to conventional norms of society would say. Marybeth and I don't subscribe to typical relationship roles. We're not monogamous or polyamorous or into bigamy or polygamy. We're just... whatever we want to be whenever we want to be it."

Despite my urge to get up and leave Luca sipping his Americano alone, this was all too strange not to investigate further. As a lawyer, I had no doubt met my share of unique or just plain weird individuals, especially during my internship with a high-profile defense attorney.

I was almost surprised I hadn't been able to sense something was off with him from the moment he sat down. But Luca seemed a different type of strange. He was a strange that usually stayed hidden until there was no avoiding revealing it—like a third nipple or a genital piercing.

"I'm pretty sure 'relationship queer' is offensive to the LGBTQ community," I said.

Luca laughed like the idea was ridiculous, like *I* was ridiculous. "I doubt that. They're an accepting group of people. Not subscribing to a particular belief regarding how relationships should be practiced is like not identifying with a particular gender. Genderqueer, *relationship* queer," he said like it was justification. "It's the same."

"It's not the same."

When Luca's phone sounded with a text, he picked it up and began typing back. "Sorry. One second. It's Marybeth wanting to know how everything's going."

I slumped back in my seat, wondering—and kind of hating myself for it—what Luca was writing back.

Fifteen minutes later, he left after telling me it wasn't going the way he planned. *No fucking kidding!* My sister was going to get an earful about this one.

"He told me he was 'relationship queer,' Liv. I think I've earned a break from this adventure for a while." I finished the last few sips of my tea and then spun the cup in my fingers.

I could tell by my sister's deflated sigh that she was disappointed, and I felt bad, but I couldn't keep going out with guys like the ones I'd met so far.

"I think you're being too picky," Olivia said.

"Not agreeing to see someone again after they tell you they have a girlfriend at home is *not* being too picky. Just like it wasn't being picky to turn down that date with the guy who said I was hot because I looked like his mother when she was young." That had actually been one of the less odd things he'd said. "It's called self-preservation. I could've ended up as a mummified corpse somewhere while he strutted around in my clothes."

"I feel like that's a reference to something, but I have no idea what."

"You're so young," I said with a shake of my head that my sister obviously couldn't see from the other end of the line.

Despite the almost ten-year age difference between us,

we had been close since Olivia was born—and closer after our parents' deaths eight years ago. How could we not be when we only had each other to rely on?

I hadn't hesitated to take custody of my teenage sister, even though it meant putting my own life on hold for a bit. I'd been focused on raising Liv and finishing my law degree and eventually pursuing my career. But I'd never focused on myself—not from a purely selfish standpoint anyway.

"And you're old," Liv joked. "I need some nieces and nephews running around my new apartment, and soon your eggs are gonna expire."

"It's been lovely talking to you, sis. Gotta go, though."

"Wait!" Liv said. "I'm kidding. Well, sort of. I do want you to find someone soon. You deserve to find a guy who'll tell you how beautiful you are and cook you dinner after you've worked all day. Someone who'll make love to you with a passion that—"

"I'm hanging up now," I said, making Liv laugh, which thankfully caused her to stop talking about my imaginary sex life. Not like there was a *real* one to speak of.

"Love you, Lala." *Lala* was what Liv used to call me when she was learning to talk, and she still employed it from time to time when she was trying to prevent me from killing her.

"Love you too," I said before ending the call and tossing my phone in my bag. I waited another minute before standing to throw my trash away.

"Sorry. I know it's none of my business, but you definitely made the right call getting rid of the psycho."

I turned toward the direction of the voice, which belonged to a man who'd been sitting a few tables away. I'd noticed him on his laptop when I was waiting for Luca to arrive but hadn't paid him much attention until now.

Though maybe I should have.

Even though he was seated, I could tell he was tall—long arms, broad shoulders, a swimmer's build with sandy-brown hair and eyes so green, they rivaled freshly cut grass on a spring afternoon.

"Oh, yeah, that guy was out there for sure. Who in their right mind thinks they can get someone to agree to date them when they already have a girlfriend?"

He raised his eyebrows in amusement. "It's ballsy, no doubt about that. But I was actually talking about the future Norman Bates."

I laughed. "Oh right, *that* psycho."

"And I wasn't trying to eavesdrop on your phone conversation. I sometimes pick up what happens in the background without meaning to. I've never been much of a music guy while I work. I start singing along, and before I know it, I've either accomplished nothing at all or worked every line of the latest Taylor Swift song into my doodling."

"Didn't peg you for a Swiftie," I said.

He shrugged. "I'm a sucker for anything with a catchy beat." He gave me a little wave. "I'm Grayson, by the way."

"Nice to meet you, Grayson. I'm Isla."

"Would you care to join me? I was just about to shut it down for the night." He pointed at his laptop.

"I should really get home. It's been a long day, but I'm sure I'll see you here again sometime."

My eyes went to his drawing as he sat back down, and I stifled a laugh. He'd sketched quite a caricature of Luca—wide eyes that were just as crazed as his hair, a goofy, childlike grin that made him look more dumb than it did innocent.

"I feel like his chin should be bigger," I offered before

flashing him a smile that I hoped let him know I found the illustration amusing. Then I turned to leave.

It took him a few seconds to respond, and it made me wonder if he was insulted or stunned. But as I reached the door, he called, "I'll keep that in mind."

CHAPTER FIVE

GRAYSON

Casting a surreptitious glance to my left, I tried to figure out where my drawing had gone wrong. I'd managed to capture the anchor tattoo on his neck as well as the jagged scar that sliced through one cheek and disappeared into his brown coiffed hair, but the drawing of Isla's date still wasn't doing the man justice.

It looked more like a caricature than a realistic rendering, though that was the fault of the man's overall aesthetic, not my drawing capabilities.

For her part, Isla was trying to look interested. I had to give the woman credit—when she committed, she went all in, despite the fact that her date likely *should* be committed. I erased the nose and tried to draw it a tad thicker as my ears strained to overhear their conversation. It was noisy in the Bean today, and I didn't appreciate it. Couldn't these people see I was trying to listen in on a date I had nothing to do with?

"And I'm really into swinging," the Fonzie-Popeye hybrid said.

Isla straightened and looked at him curiously. "Like at playgrounds?"

The laugh nearly burst out of me, but I managed to rein it in. Fonz-Popeye's—*Fonzeye's?*—lip curled. He evidently didn't find her comment funny.

"No," he nearly growled. "Like swinger parties." When Isla still looked confused, he sighed heavily. "Jesus. I like to fuck other people's girlfriends. Or wives. Whatever. And they can fuck mine if I have one."

Isla said something under her breath that I couldn't catch, but she looked a little thrown by the blunt honesty coming from across her table. "That's . . . very open-minded of you," I heard her finally say.

I couldn't bite back my smirk.

I had noticed that about Isla. She always tried to find the positive in the situation. Or at least phrase her thoughts positively. She was never rude or openly judgmental. Considering the kinds of people I currently worked with, that kind of attitude was a novelty. And I couldn't deny I was drawn to it.

Fonzeye shrugged his brown-leather-jacket-clad shoulders—even though it was in the high seventies outside. "I just like to get my rocks off. And I'm not really a one-woman kind of guy."

"Wow. Okay. That's great . . . for you . . . but I'm actually in the market for a one-woman guy, so I don't think this is going to work out."

"I kind of figured that when I saw you had a crucifix around your neck."

"A . . . what?" She looked down and grasped the pendant around her neck. "Oh, no, this is actually just a silver four-leaf clover."

"Crucifix, clover"—he shrugged again—"whatever."

Fonzeye's verbal acumen was staggering, as was his acute attention to detail.

Isla nodded slowly as if she were trying to figure out what

the hell to do with this odd creature sitting in front of her. "So, I think I'm just going to . . . go."

I raised my head at her words. She never left first, and I couldn't ignore that I was disappointed. Goddamn Fonzeye and his creepy swinger bullshit.

She stood.

He followed suit. "Yeah, I'm going to hit the head and then go downtown to the club I frequent. You have to be a member to get in."

"Hmm, fascinating," she said as she moved past him, trying like hell to avoid touching this person in any way. "Have fun."

"Always do."

And with that, Isla hightailed it out the front door as Fonzeye walked toward the back where the restrooms were.

I looked over my picture and realized what was missing. I erased his eyes and drew a large one, Cyclops-style, in their place. Above the picture I wrote, *I am Fonzeye, the Swinging Crucifix Slayer.*

I closed my book and began shutting down my laptop. I no longer had any desire or reason to stay. I noticed Fonzeye walk to the front of the shop and out the main door, and then I started packing up my messenger bag.

I jolted upright when someone plopped down into the seat across from me.

"You scared the hell out of me," I said—or maybe more like gasped—to Isla. "I thought you left."

"That's what I wanted Vlad to think."

"Stop. That wasn't his name."

"Okay, it wasn't. But I think it suits him better than Brian. So"—she made a grabbing motion with her hand—"let me see it."

"See what?" I asked.

"The picture. I saw you doodling over here. I know you drew us, and I *have* to see it."

Shit. Even though she hadn't been angry when she'd seen my drawing the last time, I still didn't want her thinking I was some stalker with a pencil. But when her date had arrived, my fingers had been itching to pick up my pencil, and I hadn't been able to resist the urge.

"How do you know I was drawing you?" I hedged.

"I guess I don't for sure, though I saw you scribbling away over here. I'm going to be super disappointed if you didn't commit that moment to paper."

I hesitated a moment before saying, "Well, I wouldn't want you to be disappointed."

When I reached into my bag, she did a little dance in her chair. It shouldn't have been as cute as it was. Opening the book, I set it down in front of her and braced myself.

Even though a lot of my focus had been on her date, I'd drawn her as well. But she'd been easier to capture. The way her hair cascaded down her back. Her aquiline features seemingly made to be drawn in profile. My pencil practically danced over the page.

Fonzeye had been drawn with harder edges and darker matter and had required more strokes on the page. And I couldn't resist adding his name.

"Oh my God, Fonzeye is *such* a better name than Vlad, even though I have no clue what it means. And you made him a cyclops. Genius."

My relief was palpable. It would've been easy for her to write me off as some creep and get me blacklisted from the Bean, but she was taking it in stride, finding the entertainment value I had intended. Which was how I found myself explaining the moniker I'd given her date, which made her laugh.

"I don't look half bad," she remarked as she handed the book back to me. "I'd rate your skills a nine out of ten."

"What? Where'd I lose a point?" The ridiculousness of my asking her to justify a score for a picture I drew of her without her permission wasn't lost on me. But whatever... pride was pride.

"You missed the nose piercing."

"Nose piercing?" I tried to recall Fonzeye's face in my mind. "Wait, you mean that pimple was a piercing?"

"Yup. A cute little stud in his nose. It complemented his neck tats perfectly."

A laugh burst out of me, and she joined in with a chuckle of her own. Relaxing back into my chair, I let myself revel in how much I enjoyed her sense of humor. It astounded me how difficult it seemed to be for her to find a suitable date. If I'd had any desire to go out with anyone, Isla would be at the top of my list.

"What are you doing with these pictures anyway? Selling them to the *New York Times*?"

I laughed. "I don't think the *New York Times* is coming to me for cartoon submissions."

I left out the fact that there had been a time when they might have come to me for photographs I'd taken, but that was another life—one I wasn't interested in bringing into my new one. But I couldn't ignore that she'd opened a door, and I'd be dumb not to walk through it.

"Would that bother you, though?" I asked.

"What? Having my disastrous dating life ridiculed in a

famous newspaper?" She was smiling, but her words made my chest ache a little anyway.

"You are definitely *not* the one who's a disaster."

She shrugged. "Eh, that's debatable. Maybe I'm just less obvious about it than the guys I've been meeting."

"Well, from my perspective, you're not the one who deserves any ridicule. But I can't deny that these would make for a pretty funny cartoon."

Scrunching up her face, she looked across the table at my open book. "Maybe. Still. I'm fine with you drawing them because I get a kick out of them. But as far as other people seeing them—I think I'd prefer to keep my dignity intact."

Well, there was that. I tried to find solace in the fact that she was okay with me still drawing her dates. Creating them took me back to how drawing used to be for me—before the need to prove myself. Before chasing success took over my every waking moment.

Hopefully I'd find inspiration soon. I needed to come up with something I could use on my paper's social media accounts. Or maybe my creativity would shrivel up and die, my soul would become a deserted wasteland, and life would cease to be worth living. Either was equally plausible.

She heaved a deep sigh before standing up. "I'd better go. I have an early morning meeting tomorrow."

I nodded. "I should probably head out soon too," I said, though I made no move to do so.

Slinging her bag over her shoulder, she looked down at me. "See you next week?"

"Definitely. And I promise not to miss any piercings."

She smiled. "You better not."

I watched her go, wishing for the first time since my life imploded that I wasn't better off alone.

CHAPTER SIX

ISLA

I tried to appear engaged, but I was failing miserably. I stared absently at a painting surrounded by red velvet ropes, but other than the fact that it was in a museum, I would have no way of knowing the piece of art was anything special. I could've created it in kindergarten if I'd been a more creative child.

The small canvas was only about two feet square and was some sort of abstract work that consisted of three shades of blue. I glanced to my right at Olivia, who was jotting some notes down in a book.

"I have a question. How can you tell what's a *real* work of art and what was done by a toddler?"

She stopped writing and raised an eyebrow at me. "Huh?"

I knew the comment made me sound judgmental and unappreciative of fine art, but it was purely asked out of ignorance.

"I mean . . . I get that these people are all famous, but if I saw this hanging on Kaitlynn's fridge, I would've thought Gracie made it."

Liv still seemed confused. "Well, yeah, she wouldn't have hung a famous painting on her fridge, so I'd think her first grader did it too if I saw it there."

"You know what I mean, don't you?"

Liv stuck her notebook in her purse and put her pen in her ponytail before laughing.

"I totally do. Who am I kidding? This class ends in three weeks, and I have no idea what makes good art."

"I didn't even know you were interested in art," I whispered as we walked around the corner.

She shrugged, and her wide-neck green shirt slid off one shoulder, revealing the top of the tattoo I tried to stop her from getting when she graduated high school—though I really had no idea why. It was a quote from a Shel Silverstein poem our mom used to read to us as a kid, so I knew she'd never regret it.

"I'm not interested in art," she said. "But I can draw well enough, and I figured it'd be an easy class at the end of the year. Also"—she looked over at me—"I kind of thought I might get to look at some male models."

"And the truth is finally revealed," I said, rolling my eyes. "You're ridiculous."

She pouted. "No. Ridiculous is me *studying* art, not creating it. I only got to see two penises the entire semester."

"Which paintings? Are they here?" I realized I sounded a little too excited and was suddenly conscious of what the elderly couple standing within earshot of us might think.

"Not paintings," she said. "If you're really that hard up, they make a thing called porn. It's right there online. It even moves."

"Don't give me that look," she added, even though she wasn't even looking at me to know what my expression was. She always knew how I'd react to things.

"I don't watch . . . porn," I said so lowly I wasn't sure the word had actually been said out loud. I'd *watched* it, a time or two, but I didn't *watch* it—present tense—and there was an important distinction to be made there. At least to me. I quickly went back to the topic at hand, hoping to calm heat radiating up my cheeks.

"Were they nude sculptures?"

"No. Not sculptures. Just nude." She removed her notebook and flipped through the packet she'd brought with her.

"What?"

"God, Isla, are you gonna make me spell it out for you in front of these old people?"

She really had no filter, and a part of me envied her for it. Smiling politely, she gave them both a wave when they looked our way, and I felt my skin flush again.

"I slept with two guys in my art class."

"Twoooo?"

"You say *two* like I said the word 'hundred' after it. It's not like I banged them both at once. Or they banged *me*. Whichever. Two isn't that many."

"Oh my God, Liv! Please be careful. There are diseases and weirdos and . . ."

"Bears, oh my," Olivia sang.

"I'm not kidding."

"You're forgetting that you're the one who got propositioned for a threesome with two men the other day. A proposition that—judging from their profile pictures, by the way—you should've accepted."

"Seriously, Liv! Did you even really know these two guys from your class? Have they been screened for STDs? Did they use condoms? Are you still on the pill? Condoms don't work a hundred percent of the time."

Olivia inhaled deeply and gave me the same look our childhood neighbor, Mrs. Hayden, gave me when she had to break the news to me that our cat got hit by a car.

"I know you're just looking out for me, and you raised me from the time I was twelve. But I'm not a child anymore."

"You know I know that." Both our voices were sadder than the conversation warranted, but somehow we'd turned a corner we hadn't expected.

Olivia grabbed my hand and gave it a quick squeeze. "I didn't mean it like that." Her eyes were teary.

I gave her a tight smile. "I know you didn't."

"It's sweet that you care about me and want to protect me," she said. "I just meant that we're sisters, and we need to share this stuff with each other. Sure, now it's just me doing the sharing, but those are the perks of being a carefree sophomore in college. And I know you didn't get to have the same experience, which is why I'm so adamant about you making up for lost time. Hopefully, when you go out on a date with someone worth seeing naked, I can hear some of your stories too."

I nearly choked out a laugh. Now that I thought about it, I'd never really shared any part of my sex life with my little sister—not that I had a sex life—and I didn't know if that was something I should be proud of. In my effort to protect her and become the role model my mother would have wanted me to be, in a lot of ways, I'd neglected to be Olivia's big sister.

Sure, there were nights we'd stayed up late talking about boys, but all those chats had to do with their dimples or their hair or why a kid asked Liv to dance one Friday night and then called her fat to his friends the following Monday.

I couldn't think of a time she'd told me about any of her

sexual partners—except for her first time—and she seemed to have more experience than I did if she'd had sex with two guys in a matter of a few months.

"I'm not sure I'll have many stories," I said, thinking how much I wished I would.

GRAYSON

Wednesdays at the Bean had become an event I looked forward to, like the good old days before DVRs and streaming services, when I had to settle into a special seat on the sofa and tune in at a specific time to see the show I'd been waiting for. Except this entertainment was live, and most times it was funnier than any episode of *The Office*.

Except for tonight.

I tried to focus on something other than Isla's face, but I found it exceptionally difficult. Not because she was too beautiful to look away—though she was—or because I was trying to read her lips as she talked—though she wasn't. I couldn't look away because Isla's expression looked weary. She didn't exactly seem annoyed. Discouraged maybe. Or emotionally worn out.

She scrolled through her phone as she sipped on a cup of hot tea. About ten minutes ago, I'd begun wondering whether the guy was going to show, because it was about twenty minutes past her standing appointment time.

Too distracted by whatever she was doing on her phone, she didn't seem to notice when I approached her. It was only when I took the seat across from her and suggested she stop swiping right that she took note of me.

Laughing, she tossed her phone on the table carelessly,

like she wouldn't have been upset if it broke. "I'm not on Tinder."

"I'm not judging," I replied.

"I guess I'm the one judging," she said. "I feel ridiculous doing this."

I paused for a second. None of it was really any of my business, but she'd brought it up, so . . . "What *is* it exactly that you're doing?"

She sighed heavily, as if she realized her comment had been a mistake and she'd have to explain it.

"You don't have to tell me if it's weird," I said.

"Oh, it's definitely weird."

"Well, now I'm intrigued." I folded my hands in front of me and leaned toward her like she was about to share the meaning of life with me. I obviously had some guesses as to what was happening. I just didn't know the *why* of it.

"It's actually not that exciting. Judging by your face, it might be a letdown."

"Try me," I said, thinking of how my life the past few months had been anything but thrilling. "Actually, hold that thought. Do you mind if I grab my things first?" I asked, pointing to the table I'd left that had all my belongings still on it. "The place is pretty crowded. I don't want to take up another table if I don't have to."

She gestured toward the other table. "By all means. It doesn't look like this Gage person is showing up anytime soon."

"It's just as well," I assured her. "Anyone named Gage is bad news. He'll probably have his cheeks pierced and be in a motorcycle jacket even though he doesn't own a motorcycle." Then I whispered, "What you don't know is, he had to Uber here because he lost his license after too much moonshine."

I headed over to get my things, and when I came back with my laptop bag, sketchbook, and coffee, she seemed more relaxed than she'd been when I'd sat down a few minutes ago.

Her arms were crossed, and she had an amused smirk on her face. "He makes it in his bathtub."

It took me a second to remember we'd just been talking about moonshine. I shook my head. "His toilet."

"That's so gross."

"So is Gage. He wears natural deodorant, so he has perpetual pit stains and smells like onions."

She stared at me for a moment before bursting out into a loud laugh. I laughed with her too, and when we both calmed down, she said, "I'm glad it's you here then instead of Gage."

"Me too," I said, trying not to think about how attracted I was to this woman. Not in a way that made me want to date her—because I didn't want to date *anyone*—but in a way that made me happy she was simply talking to me. "So what is it you're doing here exactly?"

"Opening myself up to ridicule and disappointment."

Cocking my head to the side sympathetically, I said, "Seriously."

"I blame my sister."

She then told me about how she'd spent most of her adult life raising Olivia after their parents died in a car accident, and then she focused on her law career. So her sister had made her a dating profile, insisting she do something for herself.

"Your career's for yourself, though. I definitely get pouring your heart and soul into your work if you're passionate about it." However, I had to admit, at least to myself, that it hadn't been the wisest decision for my love life.

She rested her elbow on the table and plopped her head down onto one palm. "My job's . . . difficult emotionally, to say the least. I'm a lawyer. Even though it's rewarding and fulfilling and everything a career you love should be, it's exhausting."

"I can't even imagine. It's also way more impressive than taking photos for a small-time paper and running their Instagram account that barely anyone follows." I'd hoped the comment would lighten the mood, and I was thankful when it seemed to.

"That's impressive."

"You're a horrible liar," I told her. "My goal is really to draw cartoons because apparently I'm a middle-schooler trapped in a grown man's body."

That made her laugh. "So why don't you?"

"My boss won't let me even try it until our social media following increases. Apparently that's where the money is these days." I raised an eyebrow like she might know better than me.

"Don't look at me," she said. "I can't even figure out how to use a dating app."

I chuckled, happy to get back to the topic at hand. "So are you doing this just to appease your sister, or . . . "

"I was at first, I think. But I'd be lying if I said I didn't think she was right that I needed to put myself out there and start dating. I've only had like two serious boyfriends in my life, and one was when I was a senior in high school. I have like zero point zero experience with . . . any of this."

I wondered if she knew she was blushing, and I felt bad that she was sharing all this with me, even though she was obviously doing it willingly.

"So," she said with another long sigh, "that's *my* story.

What's yours?"

I nodded slowly, realizing that I'd need to be honest if only because she had been. "Pretty boring, really. I did the whole college thing, then the career thing. I was a photojournalist in New York before this, but that didn't work with the whole marriage thing because I was traveling constantly. So she did the cheating-on-me-with-my-best-friend thing, and now I'm doing the recently-divorced-new-job-new-town thing." I waved Isla off, like telling her all of that had been no big deal. "See? Not at all interesting."

She was quiet for a few seconds, and the silence made me more uncomfortable than it probably should have. "So you're happy being single?" she asked.

"Very. I definitely need some time off from the relationship thing."

She took a sip of her tea before settling back into her chair and staring at me. I could see the wheels turning in her brain, and if I'd been drawing her, I could've pinpointed the moment the cartoon lightbulb appeared above her head.

It was right before she said, "What about the sex thing?"

"Excuse me?"

"Sorry," she apologized. "Sometimes I come off a little forward. I blame my law background, though it probably has more to do with the fact that I'm extremely socially inept. It's embarrassing, really."

I waited for her to continue, mainly because I had no idea how to respond.

"Okay, this is probably going to sound weird, but hear me out. The other day, I was out with Olivia and she was telling me that she slept with two guys from her art class this semester, and it got me thinking about how I literally have no idea what I'm doing in the bedroom." She shielded her eyes with her hands and looked at the table as she spoke. "God, I can't believe I'm telling you this."

"Are you saying you're . . . " I didn't even want to say the word.

"What? Saying I'm what?" The lightbulb flashed again. "Oh, no! I'm not a virgin!"

"I wasn't judging you if you were," I said.

"I know," she answered quickly. "I'm not, though. I've had sex. Plenty of times. But it was like really . . . vanilla? Is that the right word?"

I shrugged. "Maybe."

"It wasn't interesting or really any good, and I was thinking that eventually—hopefully—I'd find someone that I want to take things further with, and I want it to be good when that happens . . . amazing if it *can* be." She was rambling, and I was sure she knew it. But since I found it much too cute, I didn't rescue her. "Anyway, I'll just come out with it." She dropped her hands and made eye contact with me again like the gesture itself might give her the confidence she was lacking. "Would you be my sex guru?"

I wondered how someone might create an artistic representation of my expression right then—eyes bulging out three feet from my face, chin resting on the floor.

"I'm sorry, what?"

Exhaling slowly, she seemed to compose herself. "I told you it was going to sound weird."

"You did warn me."

"I figured that since you've been married before, you probably have a lot more experience than I do with . . . "

"Sex," I finished for her.

"Right. Sex."

"You realize you have less of it once you're married, right?" I joked. "And even less than that once she starts sleeping with your friend."

We both looked at each other for a tense moment, and I allowed myself to imagine what it would be like to be with this woman—to unbutton her sheer shirt and pull her tank top over her head, to suck on her tits, to feel her warmth surround me as I sank deep into her, moving slowly over her until we both exploded.

"Are you considering it?" she asked when I hadn't spoken.

"I am. I don't want any type of relationship, and I'm a guy, so . . . this arrangement could work for both of us."

Her shoulders fell a bit with an exhalation. "I feel like I should do something for *you*. Like, in exchange, I mean."

"Um, Isla, I'm pretty sure the sex itself is the reward for me. Plus, accepting something in exchange for sex makes me a prostitute."

"I'm being serious. What can I do for you? You'd be helping me, so I want to be able to help you too. I wouldn't feel right about it if I didn't reciprocate the favor."

Her choice of words had my cock jumping in my pants, but I tried to remain calm. I thought for a second, tapping my pen on my sketchbook, but I came up empty.

"What if I let you publish the cartoons of my dates on your Instagram thing? They're good. Maybe it'll get you some followers."

"Really?" The offer was appealing. Maybe it could become something. "I won't put your name in or draw your face in a way that you could be identified."

"Sounds good to me," she said, extending her hand so I could shake it.

We both nearly jumped, pulling our hands away from the other when we heard a deep voice ask, "Are you Isla?"

Neither of us spoke.

"I'm Gage. Sorry I'm so late. My Uber app was all fucked up, and I had to update my credit card or something."

At his mention of Uber, I saw Isla smirk, but she tried to cover it up by taking a drink.

"I'm sorry, do we know you?" I asked.

Gage looked confused, and he pulled out his phone. "I'm looking for my date. This woman, Isla." He held out the picture to us. "You're her, right?"

Isla shook her head.

"She's already on a date, man," I said.

He appeared genuinely apologetic. "Oh wow, I feel like an asshole. I'll let you get back to your coffee." Then he headed to the door he'd just entered and left.

A long moment of silence hung between us as we stared at each other until I said, "He had tobacco in his lip."

She dropped her head into her hands. "I know he did."

CHAPTER SEVEN

ISLA

Once Grayson agreed to my offer, I expected him to want to start immediately. I'd been internally panicking that he'd proposition me to meet him in the bathroom or the abandoned alley behind the coffee shop and regret my hasty decision to ask him to be my sex sensei.

But instead, he scribbled his number on a piece of paper and told me to take a few days to be sure I wanted to move forward with what I'd suggested. The consideration he showed made me feel instantly more at ease with the situation.

The fact was, I was hardly ever reckless. Being responsible for keeping my sister alive and off the pole had made impulsivity impossible. But I didn't want who I always had to be for her to define who I was for myself. I wanted to take this leap, and I wanted to take it with Grayson. Handsome, kind Grayson who sent me home with instructions to Google things I might want to try instead of acting like he knew best what was right for me.

When I got home, I went into my room and launched Google but quickly realized there might be things he wasn't willing to try either. And there were still other things he might be able to talk me into, because while some things *seemed* off-putting, they might not be when put into actual practice.

I mean, how could I *know* that nipple clamps weren't for me? They might sound like a medieval torture device, but what if they were really a path to orgasmic nirvana?

But I also didn't want to be wholly unprepared. Looking at my laptop critically for a second, I contemplated my next move. He said to research, but not all research had to be read. As Olivia had so graciously reminded me, some could be *watched.* Before I changed my mind, I went to a porn site and opened the categories.

This was the first time I'd put on porn with the intention of searching for things that involved kinkier elements than a guy pounding away at some perky young girl who could deep throat like she didn't have an esophagus.

The categories were a little daunting. I could probably rule out the ones that were specific to particular ethnic groups, since I was pretty sure that was something I couldn't change. Some of the pictures that accompanied the category names weren't helping matters either. Anal, for example, looked painful. And... painful. I wish I'd asked Grayson how big his dick was, because if he was that big, I was going to need a lot of prep work and possibly a pre-coital training regimen.

After clicking through categories for a bit—and coming to terms with the sheer quantity of fuck videos in the world—I finally found something I was willing to let play for more than thirty seconds. A woman was naked on pink satin sheets, a soft purple blindfold over her eyes and matching ties binding her wrists to a four-post bed. A bare-chested man in leather pants held a cat-o'-nine-tails.

I'd never thought of myself as one to be into masochism. Pain wasn't my bag—which anyone who'd ever seen me sustain a papercut could attest to. At least I didn't think it was. But the man wasn't hitting her with the torture device. Instead, he was letting the tails of it drag sensuously over her skin. The camera zoomed in so I could see goosebumps pebble her flesh. Then he would remove it for a few moments and stand above her silently.

My chest began to heave as I watched hers hitch with anticipation. The longer he waited, the more she would fidget and tremble, no doubt wondering where he was and when his ministrations would resume. The camera focused on her so that the viewer couldn't be sure when he would make contact with her again, and it made the internal muscles of my pussy clench in anticipation.

His timing was unpredictable, but eventually the cat would gently descend onto her again. As he worked her up, tickling her mercilessly as well as wordlessly, he began to change tactics. There started to be moments where he would flick the tails against her overly sensitive skin, not hard, but enough that it probably stung—like splashing freezing cold water on someone who'd been overheated.

He mostly reserved this treatment for her erogenous zones: her breasts and the soft skin on the inside of her thighs. The latter location would usually send her arching up, clearly trying to get contact with an even more sensitive part of her body.

As my heart rate sped up and my body zinged with need, there was no denying this scene did it for me. He let the tails drag over her pelvis one last time before he tossed it aside, lowered himself onto the bed between her legs, and began licking her clit. It was clear she hadn't expected it, because she let out a gasp that turned into a long moan of pleasure.

I couldn't resist the urge anymore. Pulling up the

sundress I'd worn on my date, I rubbed my fingers over where I throbbed. The first touch to my clit caused my spine to stiffen momentarily before I relaxed into the euphoric sensation. While I was no stranger to getting myself off, I hadn't felt this deep of a need to come in a long time—possibly ever.

I was alive with desire. It was like an out-of-body masturbatory experience, and I was a fan in a big way. Attempting to stay focused on the woman on the screen—who I could see was being fucked now, the man rocking into her without the pounding rhythm that seemed to dominate most heterosexual porn—was like my own version of edging.

I wanted nothing more than to screw my eyes shut and zero in on my own body and my own release. But I forced myself to watch her writhe and moan as the man fucked her with strong, measured thrusts.

When he whispered for her to come, it was like he was granting permission to us both. It was as if I'd been touched by a lightning rod with how hard I shuddered with my orgasm. I finger-fucked myself through it, making tremors dance up and down my spine for a few moments after my climax had crested.

My breath was still a bit ragged when I finally opened my eyes and looked at the couple on the screen. The man was jacking himself off on her, and as I watched his come coat her belly, I had the sudden urge to touch myself again. He then untied her and urged her to sprawl on top of him as he held her close.

As good as the orgasm had been, the sight before me left me feeling bereft. Because while sex was great—that wasn't what I was after. I hadn't let my sister make me a dating account and agreed to go on these dates so I could fuck around. No, I wanted the afterglow cuddling.

I wanted someone to still be in my bed the next morning. Someone to make breakfast with, and share work stories with, and have kids and grow old with. I wanted the goddamn white picket fence dream, and I hoped like hell becoming a sexual dynamo would help me get there. Being sexually competent and open-minded had to be a draw to men... didn't it?

It certainly couldn't hurt.

I also didn't think it could hurt to spend most of the rest of the night conducting more "research."

The next morning, when it was late enough that I thought I wouldn't wake Grayson up, I called him.

"Hello?" he answered.

"I think we need a safe word."

There was silence on the other end of the line before Grayson spoke. "I feel like 'good morning' would've been more appropriate."

He sounded groggy, like he might still be lying in bed. I tried not to imagine a sleepy-faced Grayson—hair light brown, disheveled in a way that looked a little messier than usual, dark scruff lining his jaw.

"Sorry. Good morning." And after a slight pause, "I think we need a safe word."

This time a laugh burst from him. "A safe word?"

"Yes, it's a word that I could use—or *you* too if you wanted—that—"

"I know what a safe word is, Isla." His tone was light, like the suggestion amused him more than it probably should.

"Oh. Have you... like been in a Dominant/submissive relationship before?"

"I have not."

I could practically hear him smiling.

"I'm being serious here."

"I know. It's cute."

I tried to ignore the compliment, however small it was, and stay focused.

"I did what you suggested and spent some time researching, and I honestly have no idea where to even begin identifying things I'm comfortable doing or not doing because I've never done any of them, and there are so many, soooo many things we could try, so I just figured it might be best if we picked a safe word in case one of us does something the other isn't comfortable with that we haven't discussed."

All of that had come out in one breath, and I knew it made me sound even crazier.

I left out my pornographic viewing, but he didn't need to know about that. Not yet, at least. After my video tour, I'd also Googled BDSM, which led me to discover the importance of a safe word.

"Okay," he said simply. "I do still think we should discuss some things you'd like to try. You know . . . so this arrangement can be as educational as possible. But I do agree a safe word can't hurt. Did you have one in mind?"

"Um, no. Not exactly. I hadn't gotten that far in the process. I guess I wanted to see if you thought we'd need one first. I just didn't wanna end up bound with a ball gag stuffed in my mouth and no way to tell you I wasn't comfortable with it."

Grayson laughed softly. "If you're gagged, you won't be able to use the safe word anyway."

My mouth hung open for a moment before I replied. "This is so complicated." Sighing, I tried to think of a way that all this could work. How was I supposed to explore new territory and test my boundaries without understanding the ins and outs of a world I had no experience in? But before I could vocalize any of that, Gray spoke.

"Why don't we just do something together first—nonsexual, I mean. Just to break the ice a little. We don't need to break out the anal beads just yet."

The smile spread slowly across my face, and I said, "That might be the sweetest thing any man's ever said to me."

GRAYSON

Isla was unpredictable, that much was for sure. She'd more than shocked me when she'd asked me to be her sexual Yoda, and then again when she'd jumped right from her proposition to discussing safe words and ball gags.

But after I thought about it, I couldn't say I was surprised by her choice of a getting-to-know-you activity. How could we trust each other in the bedroom if we didn't even know each other outside of it?

I'd left it in her hands to plan something because my first concern was her comfort. But as I tugged on the line the blue-haired teenage girl had attached to my harness, I silently prayed for my *own* safety.

Normally, I would've been psyched to try out an obstacle course, but this one looked like the ropes version of a traveling carnival that headed to the next town before anyone could figure out who to sue for their broken neck.

"You're brave," I told Isla.

She shrugged. "Brave, stupid... there's not much difference, is there?" It obviously wasn't a question she expected an answer to because she didn't wait for me to give one. "Besides, how bad can it be? There's a party of nine-year-old girls here."

I'd noticed. They were only a few feet away from us since we'd gotten grouped with them, and they hadn't stopped squealing and taking selfies since they'd arrived. I wasn't sure that our pairing with them had as much to do with the course's difficulty as it did our—or rather *my*—ability.

"They were just talking about what Justin Bieber's hair might taste like," I said. "They're what makes you brave?"

"Or stupid," she replied.

"You don't strike me as a stupid person. Crazy maybe, but not stupid."

The comment made her laugh, and it occurred to me that I probably shouldn't be this attracted to someone wearing a dirty helmet and so much bug spray it would put an adolescent boy's overuse of Axe to shame. But damn, could she wear the shit out of some ropes. Maybe we'd have to try out a little bondage sooner rather than later.

"Crazy, huh?"

I gave Isla a shrug. "What else would you call someone who propositions a stranger for sex in public?"

I felt her punch me in the arm before I saw it coming because my focus was on the skinny girl with the red ponytail who was currently swinging her way across the wooden rings like she'd been raised by P.T. Barnum.

"Hey," she said when her fist connected with my bicep.

"Hey what?" I laughed.

"I didn't proposition you for sex in *public*. I propositioned you in public for *sex*. There's a difference."

I smiled at her until she asked, "Why are you looking at me like that?"

"I can see why you make a good lawyer, that's all."

"Yeah, right! You were definitely thinking that I sound like a prostitute no matter how you phrase it."

"You're nothing like a prostitute." Jesus, was that what she thought I was calling her? "Besides, you picked *me* up for sex, so technically, if either of us is considered a prostitute, it'd be me. We've already gone over this."

She let her glare settle into me in a way that made me feel both uncomfortable and turned on at the same time. "Fair enough," she finally said. "You can be Julia Roberts in our situation."

She flashed me a smile before turning to approach the rings. Apparently during her stare-down, the other four girls had crossed so effortlessly, I hadn't even noticed. But I certainly didn't miss Isla's turn.

Every muscle in her back flexed around her tight racerback tank top, and I even cocked my head to the side to get a better view of her ass. It was impressive, to say the least. Her arms were taut and lean as she swung, her body as fluid and graceful as the gentle wind that blew through the branches around us.

Then it was my turn. If Isla was the wind, I was like one of those dark clouds that rolls in out of nowhere and makes people run for cover. I made it three rings before I slipped off and fell to the net below. I hoped I was better in bed than I was at the ropes course.

Thankfully, Isla wasn't too hard on me.

She told me she'd taken gymnastics from the time she was four through her sophomore year of high school, and she assured me that the little girls in our group took it too. I didn't know if she was making it up, but my ego didn't let me ask.

I was glad when some of the next obstacles were more

in my wheelhouse. It gave us a chance to talk a bit without me feeling the pressure of trying to stay alive. I told her I'd grown up outside of New York City, and she told me she'd grown up near here and a little bit more about her sister before it was our turn on the next obstacle.

It was an angled rope ladder that I climbed with ease, and then another rope we held on to as we swung to a platform. Isla and the other girls had a little more trouble than they did with the rings, but they managed to make it across.

For the last obstacle, we had to climb a rope dangling over a wall. The girls managed to get over, though they struggled. But when Isla tried, she got stuck about halfway up.

I positioned myself below her, my hands directly under her ass but not quite touching it. It'd be a lie if I said I didn't hope she slipped—if only for a split second—so I could feel her. I wasn't sure why I felt like this was a little inappropriate. I was only in this position for her safety. Or *mostly* in it for her safety. Plus, we'd be sleeping together soon. And sleeping together meant that we'd see and feel each other naked, so my spot below her was totally justified.

"How you doing up there?" I asked, hoping to take my mind off a naked Isla.

When my question didn't do it, her foot slipping off the one handhold did. Her foot sputtered against the wall before I caught it with my hands and hoisted her up a bit higher.

"Were you base on your squad in high school?" she called.

"Uh, I have no idea what that means. You mean like bass guitar or . . ."

She grabbed at the top of the wall and draped a leg over the other side. "Cheerleading."

I laughed loudly as I ascended the wall, thankful that I

could manage to do at least one thing better than the group of elementary schoolers.

"I don't dance unless I'm drunk, so that one was out. I was more of a baseball guy. I did that and swimming through high school. What about you? You do any sports? Other than gymnastics?" I added, not wanting her to think I'd forgotten.

She squinted up at me with the sun behind me. "Does debate club count?"

"I'm assuming that question is rhetorical."

She laughed as she unclipped her helmet and ran a hand through her hair, which was damp with sweat. "I was a total nerd. Braces and Coke-bottle glasses. It wasn't a pretty sight."

"I find it hard to believe there was ever a time when you weren't a pretty sight."

"I might just have to break out the pictures sometime to prove it, then. It's a good thing we met as adults, because there's no way you would've agreed to have sex with me in high school."

I raised an eyebrow at her. "Clearly you aren't familiar with high school boys' standards. Living and willing were like the only two criteria I looked for as a teenager."

"You're funny," she said, and her smile made me think she actually meant the comment as a compliment and not a sarcastic jab.

"So are you." I threw an arm over her shoulder as we walked back to the office to put our gear away. "Debate club," I said with a shake of my head.

Once all our equipment was returned, we headed to our cars. I found myself wishing I'd picked Isla up so our day didn't have to end here. But both of us were muddy and in definite need of showers anyway.

"So do we know each other well enough now?"

Her question surprised me, and I smirked at her. "You just cut to the chase, don't you?"

"It's the lawyer in me."

Leaning against my car, I dropped my backpack to the ground and crossed my arms, doing my best to keep her in suspense. "Well, I know you can do most obstacles better than me, which—now that I think about it—is even more embarrassing because you were a nerd," I joked.

"*Am* a nerd," she said.

"Well, considering I've been drawing comics of dates that aren't my own, I don't think I have much room to judge who's nerdier now."

"You could always draw your *own* dates."

"I could if I went on any."

She nodded slowly. "Right. You're not doing the relationship thing."

"Not anytime soon. Gotta wait for the PTSD to wear off. Dating someone would be like knowing there's a killer at the front door and instead of running through the backyard, I decide to let him in and then hide in an upstairs closet. I might be okay for a little while, but the ending's always the same."

She tried to suppress a laugh but failed. "Did you just compare your love life to a horror movie?"

"You wouldn't be so surprised if you knew my ex." I tried to keep my tone light, but I could feel the weight of the memories pressing on my chest as I spoke.

She took a step closer to me and brought a hand up to my cheek, holding it there for a few silent moments before she said anything. "What do you say we take your mind off all that?"

Her voice was low, raspy even, and I responded

immediately. My cock stood at attention, and I wanted to adjust it in my shorts. I inched my face closer to hers, our mouths practically touching now.

"What'd you have in mind?"

She answered with her lips, but no sound escaped them. They touched mine, and I could feel the need coursing through both of us as our tongues moved slowly over each other's. A moan came from so low in her chest, I felt it more than heard it, and it made me groan in response. I was fully hard now, and I was sure I'd stay that way until I came.

"I could get on board with this idea," I said, pulling away for just long enough to speak.

We kissed for a little longer, our hands feeling places that weren't entirely appropriate for a family-friendly parking lot, before we finally broke away. She was breathless, and I was surprised I was too. At least we had sexual chemistry. That was for sure.

"We may need showers first," Isla suggested.

Showers are overrated. "Right. That's probably a good idea."

She took a step back. "So another time?"

"We could save water and shower together," I offered, only half kidding.

Her laugh told me she was going to decline my invitation.

"Another time, then," I said. "Soon."

"Definitely soon. It'll be like getting-to-know-you sex. You know . . . before we take out the handcuffs."

"Sounds good." It also sounded like I'd be handling this hard-on myself later because this boy wasn't going down on its own. I definitely did *not* check out her ass as she walked all the way to her car across the lot. And I would *not* be picturing it later when I rubbed one out in the shower, wishing she was there.

CHAPTER EIGHT

GRAYSON

When Isla had suggested we start out with a kind of get-to-know-you romp, I had no idea it would be this nerve-racking. Even though I'd made it clear that I was just a normal guy, she still expected me to have some level of prowess in the bedroom.

When we'd agreed to meet for coffee at the Bean, and then agreed to take each other up on the sex rain check from the other day, I'd been all in. But now, with the main event looming in front of me, fear of disappointing her swamped me as we walked to my place.

Not to mention, I didn't want to fuck this up for selfish reasons as well. This was the kind of no-strings-attached arrangement most guys only dreamed about. And here it was, served up to me on a beautiful platter.

I was surprised with how much Isla was open to trying, but it was also overwhelming. It seemed daunting to try to figure out how to please her during kinkier encounters when I didn't know how her body responded to the basics. Which was why it was vitally important to have our own version of Sex 101 before we started talking about which types of rope might be best to restrain her with.

"This is me," I said as I pointed to my building. It probably wasn't the most appealing place to a successful lawyer since my apartment was situated over a hardware store, but it was clean and in a safe neighborhood. I hadn't had many other requirements when I'd left my ex-wife and moved to Monroe.

"I've walked by here a thousand times but never went inside," she replied, gesturing toward the store.

"Mr. Perkins, the guy who owns the shop, also owns my apartment upstairs. He's a nice guy, and it's helpful that he can do most repairs himself." I fumbled with my keys for a second until I found the right one and slid it into the lock, turning it until I heard the deadbolt click open. Stepping back, I gestured in front of me. "After you."

She glanced inside. "I feel like every horror movie I've ever seen starts just like this."

"I feel like we talk about our lives being horror movies a lot. Also, the villain can't kill virgins, so you're safe," I teased, which earned me a slap to the arm.

"I said I *wasn't* a virgin, jerk." She stepped inside and waited for me at the base of the stairs while I locked the door behind me.

Moving past her, I led her to the second floor where my unit was. There was still one more above me, which housed a nocturnal creature with an affinity for house music. I rarely saw him but thought his name was Glover. The way his clothes were always splattered with paint led me to believe he was an artist. When we reached my apartment, I unlocked the door quickly and threw it open as if I were ripping off a Band-Aid.

It wasn't that my place was messy or embarrassingly small. It was just... minimalistic. I hadn't had any desire to move much from my old life into my new one, so I'd commandeered my favorite recliner, an end table, and then bought an entertainment center to hold my TV. A lot of my stuff was still at my old house. Down the hall, there was a bedroom with a queen-size bed and thankfully fresh sheets.

"It's not much," I muttered as I ran a hand over the back of my head.

She walked over to the wall that held the only hint of my former self—the only indication of pride I still allowed myself to boast.

"These are beautiful," she said as she looked at the array of photographs I'd taken over the course of my career.

Joining her, I looked at my work and tried to imagine what she saw. Despite wanting my future to look different from my past, it still floored me to see the places I'd been able to go, the images I'd had the opportunity to capture. But it was also awkward as hell to accept praise for them.

"Thanks."

She studied me for a moment before turning back to the wall. She continued to appraise the framed photos but didn't comment anymore. I wasn't sure if my unease had been clear on my face or if she simply wanted to keep this train moving toward its intended destination.

Looking around, she made no mention of my sparse living space. Instead she merely said, "Show me the bedroom." It was a quiet command that gave me insight into the lawyer beneath the beautiful, demure surface. Which was why I couldn't contain my next words.

"What type of law do you practice?" It seemed a silly thing to ask, but an even sillier thing not to know. We hadn't shared a ton of words, but I was about to see her naked. It seemed only right to know a little more about her, though I could admit my timing perhaps needed work.

She looked taken aback at first, which made sense since my question had seemingly come out of thin air. "Family law."

Now it was my turn to be surprised, though I had no idea why. I'd known a lot of lawyers over the course of my life, and she didn't bleed arrogance like many of the high-profile ones who talked of mergers and acquisitions over every meal. But still, I guess I'd pictured her in that world, my mind automatically going there when she'd revealed she was a lawyer. But now that she'd told me, I could see that more easily.

At my silence, she continued. "I like helping families find out what's best for them and then helping them get to that point."

Her words could have sounded like a canned response—a reply she'd been trained to give so that she came across as sympathetic. But the genuineness couldn't be denied, and I found myself wanting to know more about this assertive do-gooder who wanted a sex practice dummy.

She was a lesson in contrasts, but I had to remind myself that I was the teacher in this scenario. And like all good teacher-student relationships, this was best kept as impersonal as possible. Well, as impersonal as fucking each other senseless would allow.

"I can see that being a good fit for you," I said because I felt I needed to say something. And it was the truth, despite my being unsure how I could truly know such a thing.

Isla offered me a small smile in return and moved closer, her breasts pressing against my upper abdomen.

"So, about your bedroom."

Her proximity . . . did things to me. My body perked up as if it were an obedient dog being offered a treat.

"Right this way," I replied hurriedly, grabbing her hand

and leading her down the hall at a near gallop.

Her laughter behind me let me know I'd done a good job breaking the weird moment we'd found ourselves in. My door was already ajar, and as we passed over the threshold, I reached for the light switch. The bedroom was as bare as the rest of my place, but it was functional for our purpose. I even thought it might be better this way—no personal touches or personality. It was a blank canvas that could easily be made into whatever we needed it to be for whatever scene she wanted to create.

I tracked her as she moved through my space, setting her bag down on a chair in the corner and taking a quick look around before settling on the bottom edge of the bed.

She leaned back on her arms and asked, "Is this awkward?"

I moved closer but didn't crowd her. "Does it feel awkward?"

"Yes and no. I think it more feels awkward because my mind *thinks* it should be."

"What does your body tell you?"

"To stop talking and get you naked."

Deciding that more action was necessary, I pulled my shirt over my head and let it drop onto the floor.

"Then maybe that's what we listen to."

A slow smile spread across her face as she fingered the bottom of her light-green tank top before slowly working it up her body and dropping it next to my shirt. Then she stood and unbuttoned her white shorts and let those fall to the ground with a gentle push. Her white bra was see-through, as was her matching thong.

I wasn't entirely sure I wanted her to take either article of clothing off, because she looked fucking fantastic in them.

The soft swell of her breasts, which weren't overly large but enough to get a handful of, and her flat stomach that led down to a pussy with only a thin trail of hair was arousing in every conceivable way.

I was lost in staring at her when she spoke. "This works better if you're naked too."

Smirking at her, I undid the button of my jeans. "Does it now?"

She didn't reply, but she didn't need to. We both knew, as the sexual tension radiated between us, that no matter how we were dressed, this would work for both of us just fine.

ISLA

Taking a deep breath through my nose, I tried to keep myself in place when all I really wanted to do was leap at him. Because *holy shit* was Gray hiding a phenomenal body under the T-shirts he always wore.

Granted, some of them had been tight enough to hint at what was beneath, but there was nothing quite like seeing the smattering of dark hair spread across a muscled chest. And his abs . . . he had abs! Well, four of them, but I was pretty sure if he dropped to the floor and did some sit-ups, the other two would come out to play as well. He was lean and trim, and I said a silent thanks to whatever deity handed out hot bodies, because I definitely hit the jackpot.

He pushed his jeans over his hips and down his compactly muscled legs before stepping out of them. He wore dark-blue boxer briefs that clung to his thighs and did nothing to hide his arousal. His *impressive* arousal. Not so big that I feared for the safety of my vagina, but certainly big enough to get the job done.

I moved my hands to my back so I could unclasp my bra, but he stepped forward quickly, putting his arms on my forearms.

"Let me," he said.

Truth be told, I'd let him do almost anything he wanted in that moment. Almost. Because I still wasn't sure about the anal or nipple clamps.

I let my arms drop as he slid his underneath mine and skimmed them around my ribs to my back, where he grasped the clasp and unhooked my bra. It slackened but didn't fall away, for which I was thankful because it caused Gray to grab the straps and slide them down my arms seductively. My skin was hypersensitive, and the soft fabric gliding over it made pinpricks burst across my skin.

My nipples hardened as they hit the air, and the fact that I was naked in front of one of the sexiest men I'd ever seen in person had heat radiating down my entire body, stopping only to linger on some of my more sensitive areas.

Grayson stood in front of me, close enough to press his erection against my abdomen, which thankfully he did before wrapping his arm around me and running his fingers up my spine softly.

"What do you like?" he rasped against my ear, making me tilt my head to the side so I could submit to him.

"This is working," I said, referring to the way his lips ran over my neck so lightly, it practically made me shiver.

His response was a low groan against my skin, and all I could think about was wrapping my hand around that cock that was pressing hard against me. I inched my hand closer, running it over his side and around his abs before making its descent.

Scratching my nails lightly just above his boxers, it took me a moment to get the nerve to touch them. He seemed to sense my hesitancy, because his hand found mine and helped guide me under the elastic waistband. Sliding my hand lower, I heard his breath hitch as his abs contracted. The realization that I was clearly doing something right had me wet and wanting.

"Feel good?" I uttered, needing to hear a verbal confirmation.

Letting out a long sigh as his hand skirted down my skin, he moaned an "Mm-hmm. So good."

We'd barely even touched each other and both of us seemed ready to explode with desire. It was all so slow, so careful, as I put my hand around his cock and he lowered my thong enough to reach my clit. But I needed more—needed faster, harder. Suddenly his gentle touch wasn't enough.

"Put your fingers inside," I said, and I felt him smile against my lips before he deepened the kiss.

I was caught off guard when he spun me around and placed me on the bed without warning, but I loved how he took control without asking permission—how he leaned next to me on one arm and used the other to remove my panties in one rough tug. They caught on my foot for a second, but he managed to free them and toss them to the side of the bed.

And just like that, his fingers were inside me, his thumb swirling over my clit with the same rhythm he used inside.

So lost in the sensation, I almost forgot I was supposed to be touching him too. But I quickly went back to his dick, freeing it fully as he shimmied out of his boxers to give me an all-access pass to the throbbing length of him. I moved my hand over him steadily, wondering if this was how he liked it but too self-conscious to ask.

I shut my eyes tighter as my body responded to his touch. Part of me was embarrassed by how wet I sounded. I could hear it—how slick his fingers were as they practically dripped with my need to come.

"God, you're sexy," he said. "Look at me." It was more of a request than a command, but that didn't make it any less hot. And when I looked into his eyes, I found myself unable to look anywhere else. "Tighter," he said, and this time it was an order. He wanted me to grip him harder, and I was more than happy to comply.

I brought my hand to his shaft, and he choked out a groan at the change in contact.

"I'm trying so hard not to come right now."

"You can if you want to."

"Ladies first." He added another finger to the equation, and I nearly lost it. Wanting the feeling to last as long as possible, I managed to hold on for another minute or so while he stroked me.

I made a mental note to ask him exactly what the hell he was doing so I could try to replicate it on my own sometime. But I knew it wouldn't feel exactly the same, because his fingers were thicker, his touch rougher than mine would ever be.

Not to mention I wouldn't have access to his scent. It made me want to buy a case of the soap, shampoo, deodorant, aftershave, and whatever else he used so I could bottle up my own concoction of Grayson cologne. I was pretty sure if I inhaled deeply enough, I could get off with only his smell. And as I nuzzled myself against his skin and breathed deeply, letting my chest rise and fall, I finally let go. I shook with my release, thoroughly enjoying the loss of control as I relinquished all of it to Grayson.

I hadn't realized how quickly I'd been jerking him, and by his heavy breaths and how thick he felt in my hand, I knew he must be close. He let me move over him for a few more seconds before abruptly grabbing my hand to stop it. His palm was large over mine, and it wrapped over the head of his cock, like he was trying to use his hand to stop the come from squirting out.

He choked out a harsh "Stop" before flipping over and setting me on top of him in one swift movement.

"Oh, this is like a thing, right? I forget what it's called, but I read about it."

"What's a thing?"

"Like when you stop right before you come."

He laughed, but it sounded more like a frustrated groan. "It's called edging."

"Yeah! Is that what you're doing?"

"I was actually just trying to stop myself from coming all over your stomach, but sure, we can go with edging."

I laughed too, and it made me even more relaxed than I already felt around him. "You're that close, huh?"

He nodded as I ground slowly over his erection, letting my own wetness lubricate him in a way that brought me quickly back to the aroused state I'd just come down from. "And if you keep doing that, I'll come all over my *own* stomach."

"I think I'd like to see that," I replied before I could censor it. I wasn't used to being this open with a man, but there was something about Grayson—or maybe our arrangement—that made most of my inhibitions disappear temporarily. I was sex drunk and enjoying every moment of it. Especially when he grabbed my hips and halted any possible movement.

"Let me get a condom," he said, reaching over to the table next to his bed.

I was surprised when he handed it to me, but I didn't hesitate to sheath him, taking my time as I rolled the latex down his shaft. I could tell he was straining as my fingers moved over him. I wanted to impale myself on him, take all of him inside me at once. But the bastard didn't let me.

He teased me—placing his head at my opening but not pushing inside. Instead, he moved it over me, bringing me closer and closer to another release. I had to remind myself how he must be feeling under me, waiting for his own relief, which I hoped would be an explosion so epic, I could feel his cock pulse inside me as he came.

"Please," I whimpered.

"You want this?"

"God, yes. In . . . side . . . now."

"You're so demanding," he teased, but thankfully, he finally filled me. Neither of us were going to last long, and it made me kind of sad until I remembered there would be more of this. More of Grayson, more of his dick, more of these orgasms that had us both shaking in the other's arms.

I wanted to go again when he finally came because it was beautiful and sexy and dirty all at once. He muttered a few soft curses and squeezed my ass in a way that seemed more reflexive than intentional. Yup, I'd definitely need more of this.

I was so sated and spent, I didn't even notice him get up. I only realized he'd gone to the bathroom when he came back. He slid back into bed beside me, and both of us lay on our backs, our eyes on the ceiling, as we listened to the silence.

Grayson was the first to speak. "So, was that . . . good?"

"Good, great, incredible," I answered.

"Really?"

I was suddenly self-conscious. Wasn't it that good for him? "Yeah, I mean, I've had better," I lied, "but it was a solid start."

"You've had better?" he said, his head falling to the side to look at me. "Tell me how to improve." His voice was urgent, as if he needed immediate feedback—some constructive criticism.

I turned my head too so I could look at him. "I'm kidding. You made me come twice in like ten minutes. I can't really ask for much more than that."

Grayson smiled. "Maybe next time I'll go for the Triple Crown."

"Did you just use a horse racing metaphor to describe our sex life?"

"I guess I did." He thought for a second and then said, "Hat trick?"

Nodding, I gave him a small kiss before I realized that might be strange.

Did people in this situation kiss or cuddle? I had no idea. *How long do we lie in bed together before it seems weird? Do we sleep over? Or does our postcoital routine consist of a quick exit without so much as a goodbye?*

This might be more complicated than I'd anticipated, and I wished I'd thought it through more thoroughly—established some ground rules before we got down to business, so to speak.

We were quiet for a few more moments before he asked, "What did you like? Or . . . not like?"

I wasn't sure there was anything that I *didn't* like, other than when it was over. And even though it was good—fucking fantastic actually—I hadn't given any thought as to why.

"I liked how you teased me," I said. "Had your fingers in me before your . . . " I placed my hand on his penis because for some reason, in my socially inept mind, that was less awkward than saying the word.

He laughed and asked, "What else?"

"The talking," I answered. "It felt . . . comfortable. And it turned me on."

Grayson smiled and ran a hand over my arm. "What else turns you on? In the past with other guys?"

"I've liked when they pinch my nipples and when guys go down on me."

"What else?"

"I'm not sure. I think that's kind of what you're here for."

"What about by yourself?"

"By myself?" I felt my cheeks heat up.

"Don't tell me you don't do that. I'm not falling for that bullshit. Every healthy adult with any sort of a sexual appetite knows how to get themselves off. Even women."

"I wasn't going to say I don't do that." I sounded defensive, and I almost laughed at the fact that I was assuring him that I masturbate instead of the other way around. "I just don't do it . . . a lot."

He gave me an amused smile. "Hmm . . . what's a lot?"

"I don't know," I replied quickly. "How often do you jerk off?"

"Depends on my schedule. Four times a week minimum, two times a day if I have more time on my hands."

I laughed at his pun, sure that it was intentional. "You're very honest," I said, though what I was thinking was, *That seems extremely time-consuming.*

His dimples became more defined with his smile. "Well,

you should probably know I usually don't talk about my masturbation habits with just any woman."

"I must be special, then."

"You're something." He smiled wider. "So are you gonna tell me?" he asked, lifting an eyebrow and rising up on his elbow, obviously excited for whatever I might reveal.

"Two? Maybe three?"

"Why do you sound unsure?"

"You ask a lot of questions."

"I was a journalist, remember?"

"Okay, that's true." I gave him a playful shove to his shoulder, wondering if photojournalists conduct interviews but being too embarrassed to ask. Which I found exceptionally strange considering I'd hired this guy as my personal sexpert and we were currently discussing our masturbatory schedules.

"My question stands. Is that the number? Two or three? A good journalist won't allow someone to dodge a question."

Grayson knew how to make me laugh, and it made it easier to be open with him.

"Off the record?"

"You have my word," he answered seriously.

"Two might be a high estimate."

I didn't know how to read the "Ooookay" that he responded with, but I didn't have to because he followed it up with, "So when was the last time?"

I was quiet for a moment as I acclimated to the warmth spreading through my body at the memory. Now that I had Grayson as my realistic fantasy, maybe I'd touch myself more often. Reaching over, he put a hand on my arm and rubbed it slowly. I wondered if he could feel the goosebumps that had popped up.

"A few days ago," I answered honestly. "When we agreed to this . . . arrangement."

That made him laugh out loud.

"What?" I said, reaching out to hit him again.

This time he grabbed my wrist. It didn't hurt, but it was firm enough to keep me from bringing my arm back to me. He held it there for a moment, probably gauging my reaction before slowly releasing it. I missed the feel of his fingers around me more than I wanted to admit out loud. At least not yet. Though that might be a conversation I'd be willing to have at a later date.

"Why'd you laugh?" I asked.

Grabbing my hips unexpectedly, he rolled me over so instead of being on my side, my back was flat against the mattress. Before I knew it, his hips were between my legs, and one of his hands pinned my smaller ones above me. His cock was hard. So, so hard. It made it tough to focus.

"I just find it coincidental that your once or twice a week happened the same day we decided to start sleeping with each other, that's all."

I exhaled heavily as he moved over me slowly. "Don't flatter yourself. You told me to do a little research, so I ended up watching porn, and—"

Nipping along my neck, he said, "I wish I'd thought to call that research when I was in middle school."

I tried to laugh, but it came out as an awkward moan. I wondered if he was going to speed up because the long, slow strokes over my drenched pussy were killing me, and his weight over me was too much for me to control the intensity of the movement. He definitely had the power, and the realization turned me on even more.

"So what'd you watch?" he groaned.

"I don't remember the name of it or anything."

"But you liked it?"

"Well, yeah. I wouldn't have watched it if I didn't."

"Tell me about it."

Not sure what he wanted to know exactly, I began, "It was male-female, which is really the only kind I've ever watched." Our breathing was heavy now, both of us grinding against the other more frantically. I craved him inside me, but he didn't have a condom on, and there was no way I'd ask him to stop what he was doing to get one. "The guy was in leather."

"You into that?" he breathed.

"I didn't think so." God, I was so close again. "But he had one of those cat-o'-nine-tails things, and he was dragging it over her body. So slowly," I huffed. "So lightly. Like a feather."

"Did it make you come?" he asked.

"Yeah." I swallowed hard, my eyes shutting as I tried to draw out the pleasure before I shattered beneath him. "You're gonna make me come too."

I barely got the words out before he told me to let go, essentially granting me the permission I didn't know I'd been waiting for. His cock moved over me, hitting my clit, my pussy, and just enough of my asshole to make me reconsider my initial thoughts on anal.

When I finally came, it was like an explosion over him. I could feel how wet I was—*hear* it—as he ground over me. I wished he'd been inside me again because the orgasm felt hollow somehow—all tingly and shaky with nothing to hold on to as my vagina pulsed.

A few seconds later, he groaned lowly as he buried his head in the crook of my neck, and I knew he was close to coming.

"Go," I told him.

At my command, he pulled back, frantically grabbing ahold of himself and pumping his fist. I was thinking about how it was the hottest thing I'd probably ever seen when he finished and warm come spilled from him, landing between my legs on the sheet.

He collapsed next to me, both of us still struggling to catch our breath. "There's my twice daily," he joked.

Letting my head roll to the side so I could look at him, I smiled. "And there's my Triple Crown."

CHAPTER NINE

GRAYSON

"I feel weird going in here," I said as I held the door for Isla to enter in front of me.

"Why? It's something we all do," she said as her head swept over the space, no doubt taking it all in.

"We all wear puppy masks and tails?" I asked as I let my hand drift over the leather paraphernalia.

"Well, maybe not that. But we all have sex." She looked over her shoulder and smiled widely. "At least *we do* now."

The memory of our first encounter together flooded through my mind, making my pants feel a bit tighter. Despite her confessed lack of experience, Isla was beautiful, fun, and clearly game for anything if our current location was any indication. The fact that she'd chosen me to go on this no-strings sexual journey with her was probably the best luck I'd ever had in my life.

"So what looks interesting to you?" I asked to get us back on track before I dragged her back to my apartment to show her how resourceful I could be with just my hands.

"I'm not—"

"Welcome to the Love Den," a deep voice said behind us. "What can I help you find today?"

We both whirled around, startled by the sudden words,

and took in the interloper. The guy in front of us was rail thin and about five-foot-five with platinum-blond hair, a mesh tank top, and tattoos covering most of his skin. Two nipple piercings poked through the holes in the material.

He oozed confidence, and it threw me off-kilter, maybe because I hadn't been expecting to see a man working here. I was supposed to be the sex guru, but being confronted with a man who worked in a shop that sold sex toys was making me self-conscious of my "sexing" abilities. *This* was the kind of guy who should be guiding Isla through her discovery. Not that I'd ever suggest that. Young, dumb, and emo would have to find his own apprentice.

Isla's eyes tracked over the man whose name tag read Cyrus. It took her a moment to refocus on his face and answer him. "We're not sure exactly. Just kind of browsing."

"That's cool." He nodded slowly, his eyes darting between us. He stood there without saying more until the moment became awkward.

An awkwardness Isla evidently felt she had to fill. "This is kind of new to us, so we thought we'd start off easy. Maybe just some vibrators and such."

"For you or him?" Cyrus asked, tossing his thumb in my direction as he spoke.

My head jolted back as if he'd clocked me in the jaw. While I suppose I knew theoretically some guys would be into vibrators—and more power to them—I'd never thought about the possibility before. It was slightly jarring to contemplate.

"Uh, me, I guess." Her words were stilted, and I hoped to hell it wasn't because she was contemplating asking if she could shove something up my ass. If so, I was going to kill this fucking kid.

"That's cool. It's not everybody's thing." His tone made it seem like he was calling me a closed-off asshole—literally. "The vibrators are along the back wall. The dildos and anal plugs are over there too."

Nodding quickly and murmuring "Thanks," I put my hand on the small of Isla's back and led her toward the back.

"*Now* do you feel weird?" I asked.

"So incredibly weird," she whispered back.

And it only got more peculiar when we arrived at the floor-to-ceiling faux-cock display. There was every size, color, and thickness imaginable. I plucked one monster off the wall and examined it.

"I feel so intimidated."

"Me too," Isla said. "Put it back before my vagina decides to wall itself off from invaders."

Barking out a laugh, I put the phallus back on the wall. Her joke broke some of the tension that had wormed its way into the moment.

She smiled at me before turning her attention back to the wall. "Which one do you want to shove up your ass?"

And the tension was back. At least until I turned and saw her fighting off a smile.

"Don't even think about it."

"Oh, I'm thinking about it. I'm also thinking about Cyrus giving you tips on how to insert it."

I groaned loudly. "God, why?"

"Please don't reference God while we're in this place. It feels blasphemous. So which one should we get?"

"I feel like that's not a decision for me to make?"

"Why not?" she asked, sounding genuinely baffled.

"Because we've already established that it's not going inside of me."

"But you'll be the one *putting* it in me, so don't you want to have a say?"

I honestly hadn't thought I'd be doing even that much. Expecting my role to be relegated to voyeur in that scenario, her words opened a whole new world of intrigue for me. My ex had never been one to experiment with sex toys—at least not with me. I knew she had a vibrator she got at her bachelorette party, but she'd never referenced using it. It struck me then that I had more intimate knowledge of Isla than I had of the woman I'd been married to for four years. And wasn't that a major mindfuck?

"What about this one?" I asked, grabbing a light purple one that was fairly slender with a slight curve at the top. If there were such things as beginner vibrators, this one looked like it would qualify.

She took it from me and studied the package. "Ooh, it has a remote."

I wasn't sure why that was exciting, but I adored her enthusiasm.

She tucked it under her arm and started moving so she could see the other offerings on the wall, stopping in front of the anal beads and letting her fingers reach out and graze them.

"We talked about trying anal. Should we get some of these to, like, warm up the area?"

"Couldn't hurt," I replied, which was a poor choice of words. Christ. "These ones?" I asked, pulling a set of smooth balls joined together by a string off the wall.

"Yeah, they look good."

I held on to them as we continued to wander. "Here are the nipple clamps," I pointed out.

She grimaced. "I'm still on the fence about those. They look... painful."

Nodding, I moved on, not wanting to dwell on thoughts of pain. I was only after pleasure during my time with Isla.

"Oh, there are those feather duster things you were talking about."

She burst out laughing. "They're not feather dusters! And when was I talking about those?"

My forehead scrunched up. "Wasn't that the porn you got off to?"

"No, that was a cat-o'-nine-tails."

Oh yeah. The cat-o'-nine-tails was frightening. I knew she had gotten off on watching someone just being gently stroked with it, but it still felt like a purchase better reserved for someone who'd firmly earned their kink card.

"Can't we use that to accomplish the same feeling?"

She walked over to the feathers and gently touched one before shrugging. "I don't see why not." Picking one up, she added, "We need a basket or something."

"I'll go grab one." I began making my way toward the front of the store, passing Cyrus, who was sitting on the counter tapping away on his phone. His head popped up when I passed.

"Need anything, man?" he asked.

It felt like there were so many things I needed, I wasn't sure how to even respond. So I simply shook my head and kept moving, grabbing a basket and hustling back to where Isla was browsing through glow-in-the-dark cock rings.

"Are these one-size-fits-all, or is there a sizing chart somewhere?" she asked, looking sincere and curious before holding the package up in front of my—well, package. I found myself looking down at her hand as if this was a totally legitimate way to choose a cock ring.

What even was my life anymore?

CHAPTER TEN

ISLA

We went back to Grayson's place after we left the Love Den. By unspoken agreement, it had seemed his apartment was going to serve as our version of the Red Room of Pain. And I say pain because for some reason I put the nipple clamps into our basket after we'd made our fourth trip around the store. There was something about them I was drawn to even though they looked like terrifying little Tyrannosaurus rex claws.

Grayson dropped our bags on his coffee table, and we both sat down on the couch so we could riffle through them.

"Where did these come from?" he asked as he held up a pack of flavored condoms.

"Cyrus threw them in as a bonus."

"Bonus for what?"

"A bonus for buying two hundred dollars' worth of stuff."

"How thoughtful," he said, his voice as dry as the Sahara.

"It was. He was nice."

Grayson had an intense dislike of our Love Den pal, and I couldn't figure out why. He'd been happy to help, especially when I'd asked him if the efficacy of the clit-and nipple-sucker set was based on real science or porn-star logic. Seemed I had a lot to learn about blood flow and how big my nipples could get.

He grunted noncommittally and continued sorting through our stash before he sank back onto the couch.

"Where do we start?"

Surveying the things on the table, I bit my lower lip. "This is going to sound crazy, but I think I want to start with the clamps."

Sitting up quickly, Grayson looked over at me. "Really? Those barely even made it home with us."

"Yeah, but they're also the things I'm most intrigued about. I feel like if I just use them, I'll know whether I'm into pain or not, and I can put that curiosity to bed."

"I think we're tackling a lot of curiosities in bed," he said with a smirk.

"You're an incredibly big dork for a sex Yoda."

"That is literally the least hot thing you could've called me."

"Don't like that one, huh?" Tapping my lip with my index finger, I pretended to think. "What about my Love Den guide?"

Grimacing, he muttered, "Makes me think of Cyrus."

"You seem a little obsessed with him. Something you want to tell me?" His glare told me there was not. "Okay, how about... Damn it, what was the word I thought of the other night... a sexpert! That's perfect." I smiled widely until I realized he wasn't laughing like I thought he would.

Rubbing his hands over his jean-clad thighs, he looked up at me intently. "You do know that I'm not a real expert, right?" I opened my mouth to respond, but he rushed on. "I mean, I've had sex. Lots of sex. I mean, not lots in a manwhore kind of way, but I *was* married, and we tried some things. Sexy things. But, I mean, what I'm trying to say is, I'm not... I don't, like, tie women up in sex dungeons and make them call me

Master or Daddy or whatever the fuck. If I had to quantify my experience level, I'd say I was proficient with room for growth, ya know? Definitely not hitting expert status."

I tried not to laugh. Honestly I did. But it slipped out, and the small giggle quickly morphed into an uncontrollable belly laugh that I had next to no control over.

He narrowed his eyes at me like he wanted to bury my body in a landfill somewhere. "I'm glad you find my confession so amusing."

He looked guarded for the first time since I'd met him, and that sobered me almost instantly. "I'm not laughing at you. I'm laughing *with* you. You just haven't started laughing yet." When my attempted joke fell flat, I turned more fully toward him and laid my hand atop his.

But he quickly shook it off. "Stop that. It makes me feel like we're in the breakup scene of a Lifetime movie."

That made me snort out a laugh again, but I was able to rein it in before it got out of control. Thankfully this time he smiled a little too.

"Gray . . . can I call you Gray? Your name is so long."

He rolled his eyes and motioned me to continue.

I took that as a yes. "Gray, I didn't mean to imply that I thought you were some kind of Dom trainer or something. I don't expect you to have all the answers. I just want someone who's willing to go looking for the answers with me." I took a deep breath, hoping my words would sink in. "I don't need someone who's an expert by other people's standards. I just need someone who's an expert by mine. Who can be *my* sexpert."

The way he stared into my eyes as if he were searching for something was oddly reassuring. He was taking this seriously, and I appreciated the hell out of his desire to make this worthwhile for me.

Finally, he nodded and turned his attention back to the table, grabbing the nipple clamps and ripping open the packaging. He spent a couple of minutes reading over the instructions before he adjusted them somehow and then turned to me.

"Give me your finger," he said.

Without hesitation, I pointed my index finger at him and watched as he hooked the clamp into my skin.

It was definitely tight and pinched a little, but wasn't what I would consider painful. "Not bad," I told him, trying to infuse nonchalance into my voice. Inside, I was feeling a little squirrelly. An index finger was a lot different from a nipple, but no guts, no glory.

"Anything else you want to try?"

"Let's give the vibrator a whirl. Get it? Whirl?"

He shook his head, but there was no hiding his smile. He opened that package as well and disappeared for a minute to clean it with the sex toy cleaner Cyrus had told us we needed. Then he returned and put in the batteries that had been included before snatching up the bottle of lube we'd gotten.

"Should we take this to the bedroom?"

"I thought you'd never ask."

Following him into the room, I wondered how to dispel the heaviness that still hovered over us. But maybe there was no getting past it. This was a turning point for us—the beginning of our journey into Sex 2.0. No more vanilla. From here on out, we'd be mixing flavors like we were Ben and Jerry.

I just hoped we didn't find out too late we were lactose intolerant.

GRAYSON

Watching her walk to the foot of my bed and then turn toward me expectantly, waiting for me to direct this show, was a heady experience. This was more pressure than I'd let myself shoulder since I'd moved to Monroe. And it was more responsibility for another person's wants and needs than I thought I'd ever take on again.

But I watched her bite her lower lip and cross her arms lightly over her stomach, I decided to get the fuck over myself. This wasn't a time for me to overthink or worry how I was being affected. None of this was about me—not really.

I tossed the toys on the bed, and in two long strides I was in front of her, putting a hand on the back of her neck and drawing her toward me so I could take her mouth with mine. The kiss wasn't tentative or slow. As soon as our lips met, I darted my tongue into her mouth and took control, making it clear who was in charge here—who would look out for whom.

One of her hands came up to clasp the wrist of the hand I had on her nape while the other clutched at my shirt. She followed my every move, never seeking to lead, but her body pliant and willing to be led. When I pressed flush against her, she pushed back against me. When I reached between us so I could pop the button on her jeans, she canted her hips so I could have the access I needed. When I stepped back so I could quickly shuck my clothing, she stood still other than moving her hands over any exposed section of skin she could reach.

There was an urgency to my movements, a *need* to be naked with her as quickly as possible. She lifted her arms when I went to pull her shirt over her head and dropped them quickly when I unhooked her bra and dragged the straps down her biceps. Her chest heaved with every breath she took, and I knew that she felt the same thing I did. The time for talking and negotiating had passed.

Now it was time to just fucking *feel*. To experience. To enjoy.

I lowered her to the bed and let my chest rub against her pebbled nipples enough to stimulate them without making her bear too much of my weight. When the time for the clamps came, I wanted her to be begging for them. While I'd been looking them over in the living room, I'd adjusted them to only make her feel slight pressure instead of a pinch.

As I rutted against her, she moaned out, "Gray," and I knew it was time. Reaching over, I grabbed the clamps and drew up to my knees. I kneaded her breasts for a moment, caressing her nipples before pinching them into hard peaks.

"Ready?" I asked.

Her hips lifted off the bed slightly so, I assumed, she could get some friction on her clit. "So ready."

Bending down, I kissed her breathless for a second before I pulled back just enough to see what I was doing. I positioned the clamp on her nipple and slowly let go so it wouldn't be jarring. When it closed on the sensitive bud, she gasped and arched her back as much as she could with me straddling her.

"Good?" I asked.

She was breathing deeply, and I wasn't entirely sure whether that was a good or bad thing. It took her a second to answer, but she finally breathed out a, "Fine. Do the other one."

But I wasn't in the mood to follow orders. So I played with the other nipple for a bit more, sucking on it while tugging gently on the string that hung from the attached clamp.

"Oh my fucking God," she groaned.

Her words made my cock jump, and I wondered if I was maybe a bit more into torture than I'd originally thought. Pre-come pearled on the tip of my cock before sliding down the side. If I didn't move this show along, I was going to come before I even got inside of her.

Attaching the second clamp the same way as I had the first elicited a similar response in Isla. She was panting and writhing beneath me, and I was almost overwhelmed by the urge to draw her like this—all blissed out and overloaded by sensation. It was hot as fuck.

Pulling gently on the strings that connected the clamps caused her eyes to widen before screwing shut. The way her hips kept rolling against my hard dick let me know that I hadn't hurt her. Or at least not in a way she wasn't into.

"How do they feel?" I whispered, my mouth hovering above hers.

"Jesus Christ, you want me to form words right now?"

I laughed but didn't otherwise respond, which prompted her to continue.

"Feels . . . feels weird and different and like I could seriously maybe come from it eventually."

That was a ringing endorsement if I'd ever heard one. I reached for the vibrator and turned it on so she could hear it while I clicked through the various settings.

"Any requests?" I asked.

"No," she exhaled. "You . . . whatever you want."

I *really* liked the sound of that. "Good answer." Giving her a quick peck on the lips and another light pull on the string made her moan louder. I sat up so I could smother the vibrator in lube before I moved so I had better access to her pussy. Selecting the setting that made it pulsate quickly, I rested it against her clit first. As soon as it made contact with the sensitive bundle of nerves, she damn near levitated off the bed.

"Please don't ever stop doing that," she whined.

Thankfully, the vibrator had a piece that would keep contact with her clit while I fucked her with the longer shaft. I changed the setting so the pace of the vibrations was a little slower before I dragged it down her crease until I was able to push it slowly into her willing body. Angling it so her clit was also in on the action, I started fucking her with the toy, slowly at first, but picking up speed as her breathing became more erratic.

Fuck, I loved this. Watching the vibrator go in and out of her body, seeing her body alight with pleasure I was in charge of giving, was making for one of the hottest sexual encounters of my life. I reached up with my free hand and tugged on the string again.

Her shoulders hunched forward, lifting her upper body off the bed momentarily before she crashed back down.

"You ready to come?" I asked her.

"So so so so ready."

"Reach down and hold the vibrator. Keep fucking yourself with it while I release the clamps." I was desperately hoping this didn't ruin the whole thing. The instructions that came with them said the real pleasure came from taking them off, when the blood flooded back into the nipples, but that it was a pleasure born from pain. I wasn't sure how Isla would react to the rush of pain though, which made this a tough call. But my gut said to go for it, so I would.

She took control of the toy between her legs, and I enjoyed

watching her slide it in and out of herself for a minute before turning my attention back to the task at hand.

"Get yourself right at the edge," I told her. "Tell me when you're there." I put my hands on the clamps, tweaking them a bit so they'd pinch a tiny bit more.

What felt like seconds later, she was groaning that she was ready.

"Take a deep breath," I ordered.

As soon as she did, I released the clamps. A choked cry came out of her before her whole body seemed to be held in suspension for a second, and then a spasm rippled through her. She threw her head back into the mattress as she climaxed, her whole body tensed and shaking.

I took back control of the vibrator, continuing to fuck her with it, though I no longer held it in contact with her clit. Watching her in obvious rapture made it impossible for me to hold off anymore. I jerked my cock with my spare hand as I slowly worked the toy in and out of her.

At some point she must have come back to herself and realized what I was doing because she whispered, "Come on me, Gray. I want to feel it."

And that was all it took. I erupted, come spurting out of me like my cock was a geyser. Letting the toy fall to the bed between her thighs, I willed myself to keep my eyes open so I could watch myself marking her.

Her fingers slipped down to where I'd come on her, and she spread it over her skin, which made my body shudder with aftershocks.

I continued milking my cock until I was sure every drop had been released. Looking down at her, I was certain I'd never seen a more debauched sight. It was fucking beautiful.

Our eyes locked, and neither of us said anything for a few long moments, content to enjoy the minute.

But eventually she sighed, smiled up at me, and said, “So, I think I really like the nipple clamps.”

I laughed before plopping down next to her, thinking about how much I really liked *her*, but not wanting to say that. Instead, I grabbed her hand and pulled it to my mouth so I could kiss it.

“Me too.”

CHAPTER ELEVEN

GRAYSON

Jessica was practically vibrating with excitement when she approached my desk. I assumed it was because she was going to thank me for convincing Mr. Thomas to let her show the professor around yesterday, so I was thrown completely off guard when she held out her phone.

"Have you checked your Instagram lately?"

"I don't have an Instagram."

"Not *yours*. I mean the paper's."

"No. Not lately."

She placed her hands flat against my desk and bent down so she could make eye contact with me even though I was focused on my computer screen.

"Well, you need to. You've gotten a ton of followers."

Taking my eyes off my work, I leaned back in my chair. "How many's a ton?"

"Two thousand eight hundred and seventy-two," she said.

"Holy shit! Really? Why?"

"Two thousand eight hundred and seventy-seven actually," Mr. Thomas said. "Must've just got a few more. Not bad for a drawing."

I tried to take his comment as a compliment, because I knew he meant it as one. He definitely seemed impressed that the paper had such a big following now.

Mr. Thomas continued, his tiny eyes alight with excitement. "Whatever it is you're doing, keep doing it."

I knew he was trying to be encouraging, but part of me was nervous that I couldn't maintain the page's success. From my research, I knew enough to know that getting likes and followers on social media depended heavily on posting content consistently—enough to keep them engaged but still wanting more.

After Isla gave me the okay to post the cartoons, I'd put up ones of the first few dates she'd been on, but I hadn't checked it since. That was over two weeks ago. The fact that I hadn't heard about any upcoming dates—and the fact that I hadn't even thought of that until Jess had told me of my sudden Instagram success—made me nervous about the sustainability of the Instagram account's success.

I shot Isla a text and asked her to meet at the Bean.

A few hours later, I handed her the cup of herbal tea she liked and wondered what the best way to make my request would be.

"So, good news," I began, and Isla's eyes beamed at me. "The paper's Instagram page is doing pretty well."

"That's great," she said, tapping her cup against mine. "Cheers."

"Yeah. It is. You're a hit. Or the weirdos you've dated are a hit rather."

After swallowing the sip of tea she'd taken, she laughed. "There was definitely some good material there."

I passed a hand through my hair and sat down at the table we'd chosen in the corner.

"Definitely. Problem is, I'm out of it. I posted all the

drawings I did already, but I need to keep up a steady stream of content." I hesitated for a moment before coming out with it. "So I was wondering if you had any other dates lined up for the near future."

"I actually don't." She shifted like the question made her uncomfortable, and it made me feel guilty for asking. She was doing me a favor by allowing me to post my cartoons, and I wasn't in a position to make requests.

"No problem," I said. "I guess if you get any, just let me know. I'll make sure to be here."

"I just haven't logged into the app in a while," she said, grabbing her phone from her bag and unlocking it. "After the last few, I figured everyone on there was a weirdo. Though I guess as far as you're concerned, that's a good thing."

I couldn't help but laugh.

She offered me the phone. "Do you want to pick this time, or should I play some dating roulette?"

I held up my hands. "I'm not choosing. I can't be responsible for what happens next. And besides, you've had such a stellar lineup so far, I don't wanna ruin your streak." Second-guessing my suggestion, I suddenly felt the need to say, "Wait, are you sure you want to do this? I don't want to force you to spend time with a bunch of whack jobs."

She was already looking at the app. "It's totally fine. Think of it as practice for the real thing. Like how getting it on with you helps me for future sexcapades."

"Oh. Thanks?" I said, more as a question than an actual expression of gratitude.

Closing her eyes, she held the phone in one hand and scrolled with her thumb.

"Did you ever do this when you were little with a globe?

Spin it without looking to see where you'd live when you grew up?"

With her eyes closed, she couldn't see me smiling.

"Yeah. I never got anywhere good though."

"Me neither." She stopped scrolling and let the page come to a stop. "Okay." She looked down briefly before clicking a button and setting her phone down. "Hunter it is. I'll let you know if he messages me."

"Oooh, Hunter. I like the sound of that. Do you think he built his own cabin in the wilderness and lives off squirrels and boiled pond water?"

She raised an eyebrow. "Maybe. Hunter sounds preppy to me, though. Like he rowed crew at his private high school and only wears designer socks."

Chuckling, I said, "Can I see what he looks like, or do I have to wait to be surprised?"

Her eyes narrowed like the question amused her. "I think I'll make you wait. We don't even know if he'll accept my request."

"True. Why wouldn't he, though?" I hadn't thought about the implications of my question before I'd asked it. But now that it was out, I wondered how Isla would interpret it. Like I was a superficial douche who only judged women on their looks? Or like I wanted to date her? Which I didn't, and the thought was probably freaking us both out. I know it was freaking *me* out. I didn't want to *date* anyone.

She still hadn't answered me. Maybe she thought the question was rhetorical. Was it? *I need to change the subject.*

"Did he look normal?"

"Don't they all look normal?"

We stared at each other for a few silent seconds before

both of our lips raised into ridiculous grins.

She spoke first. "Should I be as excited for this disaster as you are?"

"No," I answered. "Probably not."

ISLA

As I sat at the table at the Bean, my brain argued with itself about how I wanted this date to go. It would be great if this guy had potential. But it would also be great if he wore a toupee and picked his nose. Well, great for Gray, that is. I'd told Hunter that I'd be in a coral dress in case he couldn't recognize me from my picture, though I hoped he could because I'd clicked on him so quickly, I couldn't even remember what color hair he had.

Or as a person moved toward me with a wide smile, *she*?

I had to swallow my mouthful of tea quicker than I would've liked to, and it burned on the way down. Thankfully, the expression I made when a *woman* extended her hand to me and asked if I was Isla was probably masked by the face I made when I scorched the skin off my tonsils and throat.

After swallowing, I breathed deeply, preparing myself to speak to this person. Gray was going to have a field day with this, and I was happy I managed to catch myself before I shot him a glance, because I was sure I would've lost it. And I didn't want to be rude to Hunter, who was still staring at me curiously, one hand on the chair as she waited for me to confirm that I was the person she'd agreed to meet with.

"Yes, you must be Hunter," I said, offering my hand for her to have a seat.

"That's me," she said. She pointed to the counter. "Do you

mind if I grab a drink first?"

I studied her, taking in her features and build before answering. "Not at all."

She had dark hair—darker than I remembered it being in the picture now that I thought about it—and it was shaved closely on the sides with longer waves on top. Her high cheekbones and full lips were overshadowed by a broad forehead and thick eyebrows, which were hidden, at least somewhat, by black-rimmed glasses. Any hint of femininity had been disguised with more masculine features except for her smooth, honey-colored skin that was virtually flawless without a speck of facial hair. Any doubt that might have been hiding in the depths of my consciousness as to this person's gender was quickly washed away.

It struck me as a bit odd that I found her attractive—in an objective sense, of course. The sexual attraction wasn't there, which would only make my interaction with Hunter that much more interesting.

Returning to the table with a tall, clear mug of coffee, Hunter smiled at me.

"So I gotta be honest. This is kinda strange for me."

You have no idea. "This date?"

"Yeah. I've never really done any type of online dating before."

I agreed with a slow nod, thinking that if I'd met Hunter in the "wild," there was no way I'd have mistaken her for a man and agreed to go on a date with her. But here I was, sitting across from a woman who thought I was a lesbian—or at least bisexual.

"It definitely takes some getting used to."

She gave me a smile, and some of the tension I'd noticed

when we'd first met seemed to evaporate with it. "So how long have you been doing this?"

Dating women I mistake for men? Not long. "I'm pretty new to this too, actually. My little sister set me up on the dating site because apparently she's worried I'll end up a spinster surrounded by sixteen cats."

"Not a fan of felines?" she joked.

Her question made me laugh. "Not particularly. The fact that they walk on furniture after going in their litter box is too gross to get past."

"I actually never thought of that. I'll add it to the list." She laughed too. "I'm glad we're on the same page with the cats. My ex had three."

The mention of her ex reminded me that simply by sitting here, I was leading Hunter on, and I felt too bad about that not to say something.

"Hunter," I said with a disappointed sigh. "I should be honest."

She looked at me, seemingly waiting for me to continue, and for a moment, I saw the appeal in a woman. They actually listened when people spoke.

"I'm not a lesbian," I admitted, my eyelids dropping closed for a few seconds. But not wanting to look like a coward as well as an idiot, I forced them open so I could make eye contact with her.

"I'm confused. So you're bi...or just curious or something?"

It came out as a question, but I answered, "Neither of those?"

She took a sip of her coffee before settling her back against the chair again. She looked more relaxed than I'd expected.

"So then why did you want to go out?"

"I thought you were a guy." My whole body tensed like I was preparing for a blow to the stomach. Not that I thought Hunter was going to punch me—though I really couldn't have blamed her if she had. The admission made me uncomfortable, defensive. "I mean your name is one that is typically male, no offense, and you don't dress like a woman." I had to refrain from saying "No offense" again because, ironically, that seemed more offensive somehow.

Thankfully, she laughed and said, "No offense taken." I really didn't deserve this woman. We stared silently at each other before she inhaled deeply and let out a sigh. "You sure you don't wanna try the lesbian thing just once?" she said, probably only half joking. "Maybe you'll have better luck."

I couldn't help but laugh too. "I'm sure I would. The male population is a letdown." Well, most of it, anyway. "But I'm honestly so straight. Ridiculously straight. Like an arrow. Or . . . one of those metal things you use to draw lines."

"I don't know what you're talking about."

"Oh. I don't know what they're called. They have a right angle." I drew one in the air to emphasize it. "I had to use one in my mechanical drawing class in middle school, and I think construction workers use them sometimes to draw lines on the boards—"

"It really doesn't matter." She smiled, and I smiled too before we both laughed again. "I guess I'll head out, then." She went to stand.

"No, stay. Really. You came all this way. Might as well finish your coffee."

Nodding, she sat back down, and we ended up talking for another hour. Why couldn't Hunter have been a guy?

GRAYSON

Once Hunter left, I grabbed my things and headed over to where Isla remained seated. I slid the cartoon I'd drawn across the table.

"Well, it turns out it's more difficult than you'd think to illustrate an androgynous person."

Isla kept her eyes on the drawing for a few more moments before lifting them to me. A slow smile crept over her face, and gradually, it turned into a laugh.

I couldn't help but join in.

"You should make her chest bigger. She looks too masculine here."

I laughed again. "She *was* masculine."

Her head fell into her hands. "This might be the most ridiculous thing I've done in . . . well, ever."

I raised an eyebrow. "Guess a threesome's off the table then," I teased.

"Yeah, I wouldn't get your hopes up. If Patrick and Chase weren't happening, I doubt Hunter has a chance. Though I'd be lying if I said that wasn't the best date I've been on."

I widened my eyes and felt the skin around them crinkle with my smile. "Seriously? That's . . . Well, now that I think about it, that's actually not that surprising considering her competition."

"She was pretty normal. We actually had a lot in common."

"Do you have a passion for oversized flannels also?"

She balled up a piece of a napkin and threw it across the table at me. The gesture was so cute, I didn't even bother to dodge it. If I were being honest, Isla looked cute all the time—

the way she pressed her lips together as she thought of what to say next, how her freckled cheeks flushed for seemingly no reason, the way the neck of her shirt slid just over her shoulder to reveal her pale-pink bra strap. It made me wonder if her panties matched.

"If you must know, I do own several flannels. They're great to pair with scarves and boots in colder weather."

"So that's a no on the threesome, then? Just want to make sure."

She smiled more sweetly than the question should've called for. *Cute.* "That's a no on the threesome," she echoed. "I think we should focus on the twosome first."

"Oh, you do, do you?"

Nodding, she said, "Mm-hmm," slowly. Then she reached across the table toward my face, but she didn't touch it. Instead, she grabbed my collar and adjusted it. "Just fixing you."

"That might prove a more difficult task than you think," I joked. But there was more sincerity to the words than my tone let on. I was broken, and I didn't think anyone was capable of putting me back together.

"Your collar," she said, though there wasn't actually a need for her to clarify. "It was sticking up in the back."

"Thanks," I replied. "But I wasn't too worried about it since I was planning to have you take it off me later anyway."

"Oh, were you now?" she practically sang. "Tell me more about that."

My chest expanded with anticipation before I spoke. "I liked watching you last time. With the vibrator." I kept my voice down, but I still noticed her cheeks redden. She looked beside us, most likely wondering if anyone had heard me. I didn't care if they had.

She licked her lips, swallowing hard afterward, and I wanted my fucking dick in her mouth like yesterday—wanted to feel her swallowing me instead.

"I liked watching you too," she said, and I remembered how good it felt to come all over her, to mark her with the evidence of my release. I remembered how she'd asked for it—which had only turned me on more—and I'd been more than happy to comply.

"Should we take this someplace more private, then?" I suggested.

Giving me a small smile, she nodded slowly. "How about that corner table?"

And just like that I was hard.

CHAPTER TWELVE

ISLA

A few seconds later, we were situated at a table near the back, both of us on the booth side, like a new couple who can't stand to be separated by any amount of physical distance. Gray took out his computer and turned it on before excusing himself to get something to drink.

"You want anything?" he asked, and I wondered why his computer was on.

"Nothing you can buy up there." I did my best to give him a seductive smile, but I had no idea if it came across that way. Guess this was why I needed the practice.

He smiled back at me, and when he returned, he placed a cup of ice water on the table and settled himself back into the booth. My body had bolts of electricity running through it at the thought of what Gray was going to do to me here—what *we* were going to do.

Even though I'd been the one to suggest it, I'd never done anything sexual in public before, other than the occasional kiss that always made me feel a bit self-conscious. But I'd become hyperfocused and more than willing to participate in whatever Gray had planned. No one was seated directly next to us, thank God, but someone could sit down at any moment. Though I hoped like hell they didn't.

He took a long sip of water, and I watched his Adam's apple bob up and down as he swallowed. After setting it down, he leaned down to give me a kiss that was much too chaste for my liking. Though I understood why he didn't want to draw attention to us.

Neither of us spoke as Gray logged into his computer and pulled up a browser. A minute or so later, I was looking at a porn site. Inhaling sharply, I had to resist the urge to shut it closed.

"It's okay," he said. "No one can see it. Why don't you choose something?"

"Here?" I whispered. "In a coffeehouse?"

His lip quirked up into a smile. "You picked the location."

There wasn't much I could say in response, because if I was willing to fool around in a coffee shop, I should certainly be willing to watch other people fool around. Hesitating, I brought my hand up to the computer and moved my fingers over the touchpad so I could control the mouse. Some of the videos had names that didn't interest me at all, but the visuals looked enticing.

Gray plugged headphones into the computer as I scrolled through the site. "This is for you," he said. "So choose something that turns you on." Then he placed the headphones over my ears and turned to face me. Apparently while I was watching porn, he'd be watching me.

Gray leaned his elbow against the top of the booth and rested his head in it while his other hand grazed over my thigh and under the hem of my dress. Already I was prepared, my body responding in a way that had me lubricating myself in anticipation of what was about to happen.

I thought back to when Gray hovered over me, his pulsing

cock in his hand as he stroked himself, and I realized I wanted more of that. Masturbation had never been something that turned me on before then, but suddenly I had the need to see it again.

I was slightly insecure about searching for it, but since Gray's attention was entirely focused on me, I decided to go ahead and search for "male masturbation." I realized quickly I didn't want to see the guy's face. I wanted, rather, to watch a man touch himself and be able to pretend it was Grayson.

He dipped his fingers into the ice water and removed a cube, holding it between his fingers. Then he brought his hand to my thigh, running the ice along the sensitive skin to my thong. I shivered, the sensation already too much, and it made me eager for him to go further.

"Higher," I huffed out. And he complied, pulling the lace fabric over so he could access the area where I wanted him most.

Trying not to react when he entered me was nearly impossible—especially since his hand was ice cold. I managed to at least suppress the moan that would've come out had we been alone.

Finding a video that had a man who resembled Gray's body type, I pushed Play.

Gray's fingers slipped inside me so slowly, the ache in my core seemed to grow with each stroke. I wasn't even sure he could get me there like this and wondered if he was going to bring me to the edge and then leave me unsatisfied.

The video was shot from the man's point of view as he gripped himself. I could hear the lube moving over his cock as he jerked himself, and I wondered if Gray could hear how wet I was right now. I scanned our surroundings, but no one seemed to notice us. We probably just appeared to be a couple cuddling in a booth.

I watched the video, appreciating how the man pleasured himself. His groans were low and measured, and every now and then he would speed up to pull harder before choking out a few short breaths and releasing his hand.

As his cock jerked freely, I felt what I imagined he felt—a gradual build until the need to come was so great, it was nearly impossible not to. I knew Gray could feel it too because he'd slowed down until his fingers almost stopped moving completely.

"Don't stop," I said quietly enough that I hoped no one except Gray heard, though it was hard to tell with the headphones. I felt dirty watching this, having Gray touch me like this so publicly, but I needed him to keep going.

Now I understood why people got off on public sex. The thrill of getting caught only added to the physical intensity. There was a rush to the finish, but that urgency couldn't be reflected in our movements. Well, Gray's movements. I tried not to grind against his hand, but it was proving more difficult with every passing second.

It also reminded me that I hadn't touched him yet, and that realization only added to my arousal. With that thought, I brought my hand under the table and over his jeans to the bulge inside them. I wished I could see how thick he was and what it looked like with my hand wrapped around it.

I focused on the video again, enjoying how the man moved his thumb over the slick slit on his head and then brought his hand back down to the base.

He ground against my touch, and I increased the pressure to his cock as I rubbed it. Soon our need got the better of us, and I did a quick glance around to see who was watching. Everyone seemed wrapped up in their own world—one person talking on the phone, another typing on a laptop, a third chatting across the table from her. None of them seemed at all interested in us.

It gave me more confidence than I had previously, and the need to come built more quickly as we both picked up our pace, careful not to draw attention to ourselves.

Gray toyed with my clit gently, but it was enough to make me explode around him. I drew in a quick breath and shut my eyes as my orgasm spread through my whole body, making my core pulse and waves of pleasure run up my spine. It was as if the inability to make a sound made the feeling inside more intense, like the pleasure was trapped in me because I couldn't express it. Once Gray was no longer touching me, I pulled the headphones down and fixed my clothes.

My body felt like goo, like Gray could take me in his hands and mold me into whatever he wanted me to be. A few seconds passed before I realized it was my turn to make him feel as good as I did. So caught up in my own orgasm, I'd almost forgotten to focus on his. His cock still rock-hard on my palm reminded me that my attention was needed there.

"Do you wanna finish?" I whispered.

It sounded like he choked on a laugh because he couldn't quite get it to the surface. "I'd be very disappointed if I didn't."

"I meant here. In your pants," I said, though I was sure the clarification wasn't needed.

A low groan released when he cleared his throat. "You keep doing that and I don't know that I'll have much of a choice."

I paused but not for long.

"Don't stop," he said against my ear as he burrowed his face under my hair. "I'm gonna come."

And with that, I felt his hips twitch, and I was sure if we were anywhere else, the movement would've been full thrusts in my hand instead of the shallow jerks under my palm. I wished I could see him empty himself, but the discreetness of this made the encounter equally as hot as our last.

I followed Gray's lead, waiting for his hips to settle and his cock to become less firm before I removed my hand and slid out of the booth so he could go to the restroom.

As I closed the laptop, I wondered if anyone in the coffee shop had any indication that we'd just gotten each other off while they were sipping their lattes. And for the first time since we'd settled into the booth, I hoped they did.

CHAPTER THIRTEEN

ISLA

Wandering down the aisles of the grocery store, I wondered what kind of shopper I wanted to be today. Without needing to feed Liv anymore, I sometimes let my stomach do the shopping instead of my brain. And my brain was telling me to get to the cookies stat.

It had been a long week with a difficult case of a mother who was fighting with *her* mother for custody of a sweet three-year-old boy who'd been living with his grandmother since birth. His mother had gotten her shit together, though, and was ready to be a mother, even if her mother had her doubts.

To be honest, I had my doubts too. Not because the woman didn't come across as a soundly good person who wanted the best for her son—I wouldn't have taken the case if the woman's love for her son hadn't been apparent—but because there were no certainties in life. What if I fought for this woman to get custody back and she ended up not being who she appeared to be? The what-ifs made me tense and anxious and craving comfort food.

Maybe I should call Gray and see what he was up to. He could fuck the will to think right out of me. But as quickly as the thought entered my mind, I dismissed it. I didn't want to use him for sex. Well, I *was* using him for sex, but not in this way.

What we were doing was about exploration and fun, not therapy. To use sex that way seemed like an unhealthy coping mechanism and a slippery slope that could easily devolve into a disaster. And I was enough of a disaster all on my own, thank you very much.

So instead of calling, I grabbed a package of OREOs and kept it moving. Scanning the items in the aisle, I rounded the corner until my cart suddenly jerked to a stop, causing me to walk into it. I snapped my gaze up to see a man who had likely at one time or another starred in an Abercrombie & Fitch ad campaign standing in front of me. Rubbing his hip. Because I'd just run into him with my cart.

"Oh my God, I'm so sorry," I said as I walked around the metal assassin I was pushing. And then, because I'm supremely awkward, I reached out and brushed my hand down his side before realizing what I was doing and snatched it back. "Sorry," I repeated.

"It's fine. It startled me more than anything." He rose up to his full height, which was definitely over six feet tall, and looked down at me with clear blue eyes that crinkled a little at the corners. He smiled slightly, and I was almost hypnotized by his gleaming white teeth. Surely this guy wasn't an actual human?

"I'm Hunter," he said, holding his hand out toward me.

His words interrupted my staring, and I blinked at him. "No, you're not."

Shifting on his feet, he withdrew his hand and pushed his hands into the pockets of his charcoal-gray slacks. "Uh, I'm not?"

I shook my head as if to clear it to get my brain back online. "Sorry. Again. I actually just met a Hunter a couple of days ago, and so when you said you were Hunter, it threw me a little." In an attempt to salvage this meet-cute moment I was destroying, I extended my hand to him. "Isla."

He grasped my hand firmly with his and gave it a gentle shake. "Nice to meet you."

"Nice to meet you too. Though I wish the circumstances had been a little less painful."

He thankfully laughed, and I wanted to hear the sound again. It was deep, like a rich baritone. If a laugh could be polished, that was how Hunter's would be. I was struck by how different it was from Gray's rawer, grittier voice, as if his laugh had to make its way through barbed wire before it could leave his mouth.

"So do you shop here often?" he asked. We stared at each other before we both broke into more laughter. "Wow, that was an epically horrible line," he said, his tone somehow both self-deprecating and confident. Like he knew he sounded foolish but also knew no one would ever think him a fool.

"It was pretty bad. But, yes, I do shop here often."

"Me too. Well, *now*. I just moved here not so long ago."

Seemed I was getting to meet all the new boys in town. Not that I was complaining. "Then maybe I'll see you around again." I smiled with the words, hoping I was coming across coy and demure and not like a crazed cat lady. Even though I'd already established with the other Hunter that I didn't like cats.

"Yeah, maybe." His smile widened and his tone sounded hopeful, though that could've been wishful thinking on my part.

Excusing myself, I made sure to give him a wide berth as I pushed my cart around him. I filled with pride at the fact that I only looked back over my shoulder once, a pride that only grew when I saw that he hadn't moved and was still watching me.

I ignored my inner voice, which sounded suspiciously like Gray, warning me that the man could be a serial killer, and basked in the feeling that even after years in dating hibernation, I still had some appeal.

The rest of my shopping went quickly. I kept the OREOs but made better food choices after my run-in with Hunter Number Two. Well, except for the ice cream. And the jug of sweet tea. And the REESE'S Pieces I bought at checkout because ice cream was so much better when those were liberally sprinkled on top.

When I put the last item on the belt, I heard a throat clear behind me. Thinking it was someone who was impatiently waiting for me to put the little bar that separated orders on the belt, I spun around ready for war. Until I saw Hunter Number Two smiling at me in all his golden boy glory.

"I realized I didn't want to leave our next meeting to chance," he said. "Would it be possible for me to get your number so I can give you a call sometime? Or I can give you mine if you prefer."

There was no way I wanted the stress of having to be the one to reach out first, and there was also no way I wasn't going to give this man my number. The best the dating app had done for me was introduce me to a lesbian. And I guess, in a roundabout way, to Gray. But maybe this was the universe's way of making all the other bad experiences up to me—*Just kidding with the last Hunter. Here's the real one for you to enjoy.*

"Sure, I'll give you mine," I said. He withdrew his phone and then looked at me expectantly, so I recited my phone number to him. Then he texted me so I'd have his.

"Okay, well, I'd probably better get back to my shopping. But I'll call you soon," he promised.

"Sounds good."

We smiled at each other like goofballs for a moment longer before he went back to his shopping and I paid for my groceries. And as I left the store with some pep in my step, I couldn't wait to get home and call Gray. I bet a drawing of me mowing someone down with a shopping cart was something he didn't even know was missing from the paper's social media.

GRAYSON

My cell rang, and unlike most normal humans nowadays, I didn't look at the display before answering. I blamed the fact that I'd just stepped out of the shower, but the truth was, Isla was the only one who called me with any regularity recently, and I'd started to take it for granted that it was her.

"Hello," I said as I struggled to put on my boxers with one hand.

"Grayson, hi, um, hey, it's... it's Miranda." The hesitant voice of my ex-wife sliced through me like a serrated blade.

I gave up on the boxers and let them pool at my feet. But I quickly realized standing there naked while on the phone with her wasn't exactly preferable either.

"Oh. Hi."

"How have you been?"

"Does it matter?" My words weren't intended to hurt her but rather born from genuine curiosity. She hadn't seemed to care how I was when she'd been fucking my best friend, so the sentiment felt a little hollow now.

She exhaled a large put-upon sigh that had become so

regular, it had basically doubled as the soundtrack to our marriage at the end.

"I'm trying to be civil."

"Maybe you could try to be succinct. What did you need?" With the shock gone and the anger and resentment I thought I'd buried months ago bubbling back up, I decided being curt was the best course of action to get this conversation over with before it devolved into a heated exchange where we each listed all the things we hated about each other.

It wasn't quite the rousing fun I'd been thinking of when my phone had first rung and I'd assumed it was Isla.

"I was cleaning out the attic and found a box of your things. A couple photo albums from college, some old clothes that I'm assuming you kept because they meant something to you, and a few other knickknacks."

I knew the box she was talking about. The photo albums were filled with pictures of the two of us when we'd been younger. The clothes and other keepsakes were all tied up in her in some way, either because they were *from* her or I'd acquired them in her presence. There was no way she didn't know that I'd intentionally left that box behind, since I'd dragged every other thing I'd owned out of the attic.

No, there was more to this call than Miranda was letting on, but fuck all if I cared.

"Nah, none of that sounds like anything I need. Maybe *Dennis* could fit in some of the clothes." The urge to mention his name, to speak of the thing she'd kept secret for over a year, was something I couldn't repress.

This time, her sigh was less agitated and more sad. "Why do you always have to say his name like that?"

"Like what?"

"Like he's a disease or something."

"If the inflection fits," I muttered.

"We were all friends for a lot of years, Grayson. We could—"

"If you say we could all be friends again, I'm hanging up."

"Always so dramatic."

That was a point I couldn't necessarily argue, so I didn't bother trying. I was an artist—wasn't making something from nothing kind of our whole purpose?

"Anything else?" I asked.

"No. No, I guess not." The sadness was still there, and not too long ago it would've eaten at me to know what was upsetting her. I hadn't always been the most present husband, but I'd always cared about her. If I could have fixed a problem for her, I would've. But when the problem became me, there was little I could do. Or maybe just little I was *willing* to do. Either way, the result was the same.

"Okay, then. Take care of yourself."

"Bye, Grayson."

I disconnected the call and tossed the phone on my bed. After finishing dressing, I walked into the kitchen and opened the refrigerator. Then I slammed the door shut because I refused to let Miranda drive me to stress eating.

I was . . . unsettled. One conversation with her, and all the feelings I'd tried to bury rose up and clouded my brain. What I needed was a distraction, preferably of the beautiful, black-haired variety. Returning to my room, I picked up my phone and fired off a text to Isla.

What are you up to?

The reply came almost immediately.

Plotting whether my stomach will revolt if I eat an entire carton of ice cream for dinner.

Come share it with me!

Hmm, that is a tempting offer. However, I have become one with my couch, and moving doesn't hold much appeal.

Ugh, come on. I need someone to get my mind off things.

What things?

Ex-wife things.

And then because being transparent might tip the scales of her coming over in my favor, I added:

She called me a little while ago.

While I had been expecting Isla to sympathize with me, what I didn't expect was for my phone to ring. In the interest of caution, I made sure it was her before I answered.

"To what do I owe the pleasure?"

"So . . . a chat with the ex, huh? How'd that go?"

"About as well as attempting to baptize Rosemary's baby."

"Stop deflecting with humor. Tell me."

And damn her for knowing I did that, and damn me for liking that she knew. "It's tough . . . hearing from her. There are a lot of hurt feelings between us." When she didn't say anything, I sighed and rubbed my forehead with my hand. "It's too complicated to get into. Especially over the phone."

"Okay."

"Okay?" I'd expected her to push. A masochistic part of me might even admit to hoping she would have.

"Yeah. Okay." She sounded like she was struggling.

"What are you doing?" I asked.

"Getting dressed. I'll be there in fifteen minutes. With ice cream *and* wine. Be ready to share all the sordid details." Then she hung up, leaving me staring at the phone, wondering how I'd both gotten exactly what I wanted and what I didn't all at once.

CHAPTER FOURTEEN

ISLA

The trip to Gray's was quick, and I found him waiting outside for me when I arrived.

"Such a gentleman," I said with a teasing smile.

"I wanted to make sure nothing happened to the ice cream," he deadpanned as he held the door open so I could walk inside.

"Hey, don't forget about the wine."

He closed the door behind us and I waited for him to lead the way up the stairs.

"Trust me, I'm not."

We trekked the rest of the way to his apartment in silence. Once inside, I put the ice cream in the freezer, dropped the REESE'S Pieces onto the counter, and then withdrew the wine from the bag I'd put it in.

"Where's your opener?"

He wordlessly retrieved that as well as two glasses and set them down in front of me. I poured us some wine and handed him one before saying, "Spill."

"The wine? That seems very wasteful."

"Smartass. The phone call. I need the deets."

"Deets? Are you fourteen?"

"If I were, you'd probably be looking at a long prison

term." Taking a sip of my wine, I watched him chuckle. "Stop trying to change the subject."

"It really isn't a big deal. It definitely didn't need a sugar and alcohol intervention," he said right before taking a drink.

"Then give it back," I said, making grabby hands at his glass.

"Not on your life," he muttered, draining his glass and then grabbing the bottle to refill it.

"See! This is a problem that requires drinking."

"It's not a problem at all. More of a nuisance." He sighed. "I haven't heard from Miranda since I moved here. It was just . . . jarring. To hear her voice. The past few weeks have felt like a whole new life for me, and it was weird to have my old life collide with my new one."

It was on the tip of my tongue to ask him what was different about the last few weeks. Not because I didn't think I had a role in the change, but because the selfish part of me wanted to hear it from him. But this moment wasn't about me, so I let the question drop.

"That makes sense."

"She's . . . Miranda was my first love. We met in college, and things were great for years. Until they weren't. I don't even know exactly how or when they went bad. But before I knew it, I was accepting every job that was sent my way to keep myself busy and away from home, and she was fucking my best friend Dennis every chance she got."

"That's . . . wow."

He rubbed his forehead with his hand, something I'd begun to think of as a very Gray thing to do. "We both played a part in the marriage failing. But her fucking around with him of all people, it was a double-edged betrayal."

Nodding, I thought about how glad I was that I'd never been mistreated like that. I'd had a tough life with my parents dying and having to raise Liv on my own, but no one had chosen to hurt me. Somehow that thought eased a bit of the ache inside of me that I'd carried around since the day I lost my parents. If they could've picked whether to go or stay, they would have stayed. And there was solace to be found in that truth.

"They sound like real gems."

"I thought they were—once."

"I mean, let's be honest, nothing good ever comes out of a guy named Dennis."

Gray had been taking a sip of his wine, and he snorted and choked slightly at my words.

"Seriously," I continued. "Dennis the Menace, Dennis Rodman, Dennis Nilsen—"

"Who the hell is Dennis Nilsen?"

"He's a serial killer from England or Scotland. Somewhere like that. He killed his victims and then dismembered them. I think he got off on it sexually, but that part's fuzzy."

His expression was somewhat horrified. "How do you know that?"

Shrugging, I poured myself more wine. "I'm a fount of useless knowledge. And I'm really into serial killers. I mean, not *into them* into them. I don't want to date one or anything."

"Maybe you're the one who needs an intervention."

Raising my glass as a salute, I said, "From your mouth to God's ears." Then I put my glass down excitedly. "Oh! But I may have already gotten one."

"An intervention?"

"Yes. Whether or not it was divine or not remains to be

seen, but there was some very definite intervening today. I met a guy. Another Hunter, but this one is actually a man."

He looked bewildered and entertained all at once. "How'd you meet him?"

"I ran him over with my shopping cart."

"Way to make a strong first impression."

"I know, right? I bungled the entire ordeal. But he asked for my number anyway, so maybe he likes his women easily flusterable."

"If you're going to start inventing words, I'm going to have to cut you off." He reached for my wineglass, but I smacked his hand away.

"Don't touch or I won't tell you the rest of the story."

Withdrawing his hand, he leaned on his counter, giving me his rapt attention.

After thinking for a moment, I deflated. "I guess there isn't any more to the story. We exchanged numbers, but he hasn't texted me yet. We just met a couple of hours ago."

"You could always text him."

I scoffed. "I'm not that desperate."

Gray raised his eyebrows at me.

Rolling my eyes, I grabbed my purse from where I'd dropped it on the floor and began to dig through it for my phone.

"What should I say?" I asked, my voice resigned.

Laughing, he grabbed my glass and started walking toward the living room, correctly figuring I'd follow my wine anywhere.

"I'm just fucking with you," he said. "You can wait for him to make contact first."

"What if he doesn't?"

"Then he's a fucking moron," Gray replied, his tone resolute.

His words made a warmth spread through me. I was glad I'd met this relationship-phobic man who fucked like a dream. He was turning out to be a damn good friend. Tossing my phone onto the coffee table, I swung my head to look at him.

"What should we do now? Wanna talk about your ex-wife more?"

He shuddered. "Hell no."

I smiled at his theatrics, settling back into his couch. We didn't talk for a couple of minutes, but I didn't feel any need to fill the quiet. But evidently he did.

"Wanna try the feathers?" he asked.

My smile widened. "Now you're talking."

GRAYSON

I hadn't intended to make tonight about sex, but having Isla in my space forced my mind, and body, in that direction. Besides, we did buy the feather duster thing. It would be a shame for it to go to waste. Especially if this new Hunter guy she'd met had half a brain cell and called her soon. Who knew how much longer I'd have to spend with her.

And while I didn't want it to seem like I was trying to get my fill of her before she moved on, I kind of was. Not only sexually, but personally too. I enjoyed her company as much as I enjoyed sleeping with her, and I was going to soak both up while she'd let me.

She drank what was left in her glass and stood, waiting for me to do the same. Then she led the way to my bedroom, already beginning to undress as she walked down the hall.

Dropping her clothes as she removed them, it was like following X-rated breadcrumbs. When she arrived at the foot of my bed, she turned, her hands in the waistband of her light-blue thong.

"On or off?" she asked.

"Uh . . ." Did she really expect me to be able to answer questions right now? Rubbing my palm over my hardening cock, I tried to figure out how I envisioned this going. "On."

A quirk of her eyebrows and smile told me she liked that idea. She climbed onto the bed until she sat against the headboard.

"Now what?" she asked.

Now I utterly scandalize you. "One sec," I murmured as I moved toward my closet, where I'd put the things we'd bought into one of my suitcases. We'd decided we'd be better off keeping them at my place since she'd get the most use out of them when we were together.

"Oh my God, do you have a treasure chest of sex toys in your closet?"

I panned slowly to see her leaning forward on the bed so she could peer into my closet. "What else was I supposed to do with them? Display them around the room?"

"It would bring a little something extra to your decorating style."

"What's wrong with my decorating?"

"Other than the complete and utter lack of it? Nothing."

"Is this really what you want to argue about right now?"

"No, no, as you were," she answered as she moved back into her original position, with her back against the headboard.

I looked through the contents until I found what I was looking for, and then I returned to the bed, placing the items beside her so she could see what I had planned.

"This okay with you?"

"Yup. Totally okay. Perhaps the okayest I've ever been."

I laughed as I leaned over her so I could press a soft kiss to her lips. "There you go making up words again," I murmured.

"Maybe it's not the alcohol that has that effect on me. Maybe it's you."

Moving back so I could look down at her beautiful face and into her expressive eyes, I felt an affection for this witty, intelligent woman who would have men falling all over her once she realized her appeal. It was something a dating app could never capture or convey. There was an energy about her that people needed to feel to understand.

Isla was someone who needed to be experienced. Not sexually—though that was quite a bonus—but personally. I felt like a different man just hovering in her orbit: lighter and happier. And some lucky guy was going to get a lifetime full of that feeling one day. I hoped he'd know how fucking lucky he was.

Bending down, I pressed my lips to hers and she opened for me, letting my tongue tangle with hers until I found the will to pull back. I reached over and picked up the fuzzy handcuffs we'd bought and then gently took hold of one of her wrists. Hesitating for a second, I gave her time to decide this wasn't what she wanted.

But there was no doubt or reserve anywhere on her face. Instead, she sank lower onto the bed so her back was flush against the mattress. Fastening the cuff to her wrist, I brought it over her head so I could thread the other end of the cuffs through the slats in my headboard. Once that was done, I closed the cuff around her other wrist.

She squirmed for a second, seemingly to find a comfortable position, and then gave a tug to test the strength of the cuffs. If she pulled hard enough, she might be able to break the thin slats, but they were strong enough for our purposes. Next, I took the blindfold we'd purchased and placed it over her eyes, lifting her head slightly to slide the string into place.

"Still the okayest you've ever been?" I asked, my voice pitched lower than I ever remembered hearing it.

"Yes." Her answer was clear and concise. Consenting.

I moved back from the bed and let myself take her in. There she was, all spread out, willing and waiting for whatever came next. It was one of the biggest turn-ons I'd ever experienced.

The longer I looked, the more she began to fidget. It was as if she was anticipating what she knew was coming—the fact that she had no clue *when* it was coming was making her more restless and anxious.

Trying to move as noiselessly as possible, I picked up the feathers from the bed and slid them over my palm. As the soft tickles flickered across my skin, I knew I was going to enjoy watching them glide over her body.

To start, I let the feathers hover above her flat belly and brought them down just enough to make only the slightest contact with her. I slid them over toward her hip, loving the way her breath hitched and the goosebumps I left in my wake. Moving next to the inside of her knee, I gently skimmed the feathers up the inside of her thigh, over her panties, and then up all the way to her breasts, where I let them flutter over her nipples, making them hard and pebbled. When she was practically panting from my ministrations, her body unable to stay still, I removed the feathers from her body and waited.

She practically whined at the loss and began to writhe

even harder, as if her body was seeking out contact with something, anything. When she'd calmed a bit, I began again, dancing the feather over the inside of her arm, down her torso, faintly brushing her breasts again as I passed them. There was no part of her body I hadn't sensitized with the feathers.

Every time I picked up the feathers and brought them down somewhere new, she would shrink away from them before leaning into the soft caress it offered. It was like watching the tide roll in and out, a gentle sway that was hypnotic.

"Please," she whimpered, arching her back in a way that sent her breasts higher, pushing them into where I swirled the feathers.

As hot as this was, and as much as I loved her giving me this much control, I was becoming overwhelmed with the need to touch her myself. To watch *my* fingers slide over her skin. To have her push up into my hands, craving the sensations I could bring her.

Eventually, I couldn't hold back any longer, and I let my fingers pinch her nipple while I rubbed the feathers over her clit. Her gasp morphed into a moan that caused my dick to harden further. I took advantage of my unfettered access to her body to touch her everywhere. The feathers were soon forgotten as both of my hands paid homage to the exposed skin in front of me.

"Please," she begged again. "Gray, please."

"What do you need?" I asked right before I bent to suck her nipple into my mouth.

"Oh God. I—I need . . . I need you to fuck me. Hard."

Hearing the dirty words from this beautiful woman was almost my undoing. My cock throbbed in my pants, and

I worried for the first time since I was fourteen that I might *accidentally* come in my pants, since the time at the Bean couldn't be chalked up to an accident. Quickly, I shucked my clothing and retrieved a condom from the drawer of my bedside table, rolling it down my length.

The bed dipped under my weight as I leaned on it to peel her thong down her legs. Then I climbed between her thighs and stared down at her, her hands still bound above her head, her eyes still covered by the mask.

"So beautiful," I murmured as I brought my hands up her thighs until gripping the juncture between her legs and her pelvis.

She squirmed as if trying to inch my hands higher, but my grip stayed firm. "Goddammit, Gray, stop messing around and get inside of me."

I chuckled at her whining order. Leaving her hanging for a bit longer was torture for both of us, but I managed until I couldn't hold back any more. I leaned forward so that my cock slid into her crease, and I thrust against her, turning her into a babbling mess beneath me. Then, when I thought she was near tears from the torment, I lined myself up and slid home.

The tight heat of her body hugged my straining cock so perfectly, I had to wrestle myself back from the brink of orgasm. Once I had myself under control, I began thrusting, knowing this was likely to be over quickly for both of us. I circled my thumb on her clit as I snapped my hips, driving forward into the soft wetness.

"Close," she whispered.

I doubled my efforts, driving my cock as deep as I could until I felt her shudder and convulse on me. I continued to rub her clit and thrust into her in an effort to draw her orgasm out as long as it could go. When her body relaxed, I dropped both hands to her thighs and pushed into her three more times before my own release barreled through me. It was as though every muscle in my body locked up as I emptied into the condom.

My thrusts grew shallow as I attempted to wring every drop of my orgasm. Releasing her legs, I let myself fall forward onto my hands as I caught my breath.

When I could finally form coherent words, I asked, "So . . . what did you think of the feathers?"

She lifted her arm as best she could with the cuffs and gave me a thumbs-up sign before letting it go lax again as if the act of lifting it had zapped what remaining energy she'd possessed.

"A-plus," she said, her voice sounding still slightly out of breath. "No room for improvement."

Chuckling, I bent down to give her a soft kiss on her lips and released her from the handcuffs. "*No* room for improvement? That actually sounds like a challenge."

A smile spread across her lips, and she reached up and put her hands on my cheeks. Drawing me down so she could kiss me, she said, "Bring it on."

CHAPTER FIFTEEN

ISLA

Hunter had texted me the day after we met and asked if I would like to get together with him for coffee or a drink. Since I was already nervous about the prospect of going on a date with someone I could actually be interested in, I figured adding alcohol to that mix could be disastrous for me. So I'd said coffee would be great and that I knew just the place. We were meeting at the Bean in two hours. Plenty of time to get ready and make it over there.

Except for the fact that I was freaking the hell out.

"I seriously don't get you," Liv said from where she lay sprawled on her stomach atop my bed. "You weren't nervous before your other dates. At least you know this guy isn't an ax murderer."

"How would I know that?" I muttered as I dug around for a suitable outfit.

"God, you're so literal. I just mean that you're not going into this one totally blind. You know he's attractive. And that he's a guy, which is a step in the right direction."

"Honestly, I wish I was bi. Girl Hunter had a lot to offer." My voice sounded wistful even to my own ears. "I need a whole new wardrobe. Like, what even *is* my sense of style?"

"Do you want me to actually answer that, or . . . ?"

"No, just... shh. Let me have my breakdown in peace."

"Put on a maxi dress and call it a day. It's just coffee."

But it wasn't *just* coffee. It was potentially my last first date. This could be the turning point of my entire life. Years from now, when I told the story of this night to our hypothetical children, I wanted to speak about how it was love at first sight... or second sight in our case. I wanted the story to be full of magic and fairy tales. An unbreakable bond formed over coffee and possibly a blueberry muffin. It would be the stuff of legends.

Jesus Christ, I'm really losing it. "I need to make a call," I said abruptly as I left my closet and practically ran into the bathroom.

"Don't cancel on him!" Liv yelled behind me.

Slamming the door shut, I leaned against it and found the number I needed.

"Hey, aren't you—"

"I don't have clothes," I blurted out, not caring that I'd interrupted Gray or made no sense. He wouldn't care about either one.

"Okay," he said, drawing out the first syllable. "I feel like that's an exaggeration since I have seen you in clothes on numerous occasions. Though seeing you without them is definitely my preference. But maybe you want to save nudity for at least date three."

"I don't... What do I wear?"

"You realize you're smoking hot, right? You could wear a burlap sack and it would look good."

"Don't be sweet right now. I need honesty."

"First of all, don't call me sweet. I'm not a puppy. Second, I'm always honest."

I knew this to be true, but it wasn't helping me right now. "I need you to agree that I have no clothes and therefore cannot go on this date. God, why can't you be more supportive?"

"Supportive of your neuropathy?"

"Yes."

"Isla, what's going on? This isn't you. You're one of the most confident people I know."

"You must not know many people," I mumbled. When he didn't respond, I continued. "I'm confident about doing my job and being a good person and useless crap like that. This dating stuff is way out of my scope."

"You've been going on dates for months."

"But those were doomed to fail." As the words left my mouth, I was overwhelmed by how true they were. I walked into those meetings already believing they weren't going to work out. It wasn't a conscious thought, but it colored all the dates just the same. Feeling like I was risking nothing had made it easy to interact with those men—and woman—but now I felt bad that I hadn't given them more of a chance. "I'm a bad person."

"No, you're not. You're a great person who has had to play a safe game for most of your adult life because someone else was depending on you. But this, jeopardizing your time and maybe your heart, is risky. It makes sense that it scares you a little."

"A lot. It scares me a lot." Tears prickled my eyes. Of course Gray got it. He *always* got me.

"That's totally normal. But you can't let that fear stop you. You're going on that date if I have to come over there and tickle you out of the house with those feathers."

My laughter sounded wet as it came out through the tears

slipping down my cheeks. "Are you going to be there?"

"I was planning on it. Unless you'd rather I didn't." His voice sounded unsure, and I rushed to alleviate his concern.

"No, no, I want you there. I was just making sure." When I'd originally invited him, it was because I'd wanted him to get the opportunity to sketch the date. But now the thought of him not being there made my stomach hurt.

"Then I'll be there."

"Me too," I said.

"Good." I heard the smile in his voice, and it was enough to convince me that I could do this.

We said quick goodbyes, and I hung up, lowering my phone and moving so I could see myself in the mirror. "Okay, Isla," I said to my reflection. "You got this. You are a dating ninja with voodoo skills, and none of what's coming out of your mouth makes any sense, but it doesn't even matter because it's just a date and everything will be fine."

Giving myself a final nod, I left the bathroom and returned to my bedroom, where my sister had pulled out a casual yellow-and-blue striped dress with white sandals.

"What do you think of this?" she asked.

"It's perfect."

GRAYSON

As I walked down the sidewalk toward the Bean, my messenger bag slapping against my thigh, I found myself more anxious than eager. Normally, there was a thrum of excitement in finding out who Isla had agreed to a coffee date with, to see that person and sketch him and, well, judge him. Or her.

But this time felt different. It had started with her nerve-racked phone call, though I had to admit, my reticence had been there even before I'd had to talk her down from the metaphorical ledge. Isla was excited for this date, even if she was driving herself batshit crazy in preparation for it. And her excitement made me... less so. Which was bullshit. She deserved better from me than that.

Throwing open the door of the coffeehouse, I hoped for the best. Then I ordered a cappuccino, waited while they made it, and then took my normal seat by the far wall. Scanning the room, I didn't see anyone I thought could be this Hunter character unless Isla had grown a penchant for paunchy, balding men or had decided to try her luck with more women. I was thankful my seat gave me a full view of the door so I'd be able to see this guy arrive.

Removing my sketchbook and a pencil from my bag, I opened to a fresh page and attempted to look busy while I really watched the door obsessively with only my peripheral vision. I had only arrived about ten minutes early, so unless he was a scumbag who showed up late to first dates, he'd be here any minute.

No sooner had I mentally called the guy a scumbag than a blond Adonis walked into the Bean. *For fuck's sake, is this Hunter?* The guy looked like he should be in a magazine, with his tailored slacks and lavender polo. Seriously, what kind of guy could pull off a lavender polo? I would've looked like I belonged in a Crayola box if I'd put that thing on. I watched Hunter scan the room, and when he didn't see Isla, he settled in a seat toward the front of the place.

I hadn't formed a contingency plan for what would happen if Isla didn't get there first and pick her normal seat.

Now Hunter's back was to me so he could face the door, and I found myself irrationally irritated with him for messing up our normal arrangement.

It dawned on me that I almost considered Isla and me as a team *against* her dates. Well, *against* was maybe a strong word, but that sentiment remained the same.

I'd seemed to lose sight along the way somewhere that *I* was the actual third party in all this. Isla was trying to make a go of it with one of these guys, and I was the creep who drew them striking out. My sketches weren't the core goal of these dates—at least not for her. Jesus, I was a real fucking narcissist sometimes.

While I sat here mentally berating myself, I heard the chime above the door sound, and I watched Isla walk in. I wished I could've seen Hunter's face when she arrived. Wished I could've made sure he was as taken with her as she deserved to be. Maybe that was a superficial thought, but whatever.

Isla walked in and noticed Hunter almost immediately, her eyes lighting up and a smile spreading across her face. I thought I saw her gaze dart to me, but that might have been wishful thinking. They did an awkward dance when she reached him, a should-we-hug-should-we-shake-hands kind of waltz that was endearing in its lack of coordination. She laughed brightly and they hugged—a brief, friendly infiltration of personal space—before he gestured toward the counter, no doubt asking what she wanted to drink.

After he'd walked away, her eyes strayed to me again, and I offered her a small smile—a slight tilting of lips that seemed to relax her further because her shoulders dropped a bit lower and she sat back in her chair.

I let my eyes linger on her for a moment, taking in the way

the blue-and-yellow dress showed off her figure without being too clingy, how her dark hair was tucked adorably behind her ear on one side, appreciating the porcelain skin I had mapped with my fingers and the bow of her lips that I had outlined with my tongue.

Catching myself staring, I ducked my head and picked up my pencil, bringing the point to paper and losing myself in the task of drawing before I lost myself in something much deeper. Something scarier. Something better off stopped before it had a chance to start.

CHAPTER SIXTEEN

ISLA

I couldn't help shooting another glance at Gray while I waited for Hunter to return with my iced coffee. His hand was flying over his sketchbook, as if he were desperate to get his vision out of his mind and onto the paper. He looked good like that, all engrossed in his art, the tip of his tongue poking ever so slightly out of the corner of his mouth as he concentrated. It was cute.

Hunter set my drink in front of me before claiming the seat across from me. The thought struck me that we weren't in the best position for Gray to capture the moment, but with the way he was drawing, he didn't seem to be hampered. Besides, this date wasn't about Gray's drawing. It was about getting to know Hunter, the sexy-as-sin man who was looking at me intently.

As if with a synchronized revelation, we both realized this date needed actual words to be exchanged. Well, at least ones beyond "hello" and "what can I get you to drink?"

"So, do you come here often?" he asked. He immediately followed his own question with a shake of his head and a self-deprecating laugh. "I can't believe I asked that again."

I laughed politely and said, "It's fine. And yes, I do come here fairly often." Leaving it at that in case he *was* an ax murderer who I didn't want to know the neighborhood I lived in, I tried to change the subject. "What do you do? For a living, I mean, not in general. Though I guess that's obvious. People only ask that question when they want to know what your job is. Oh, but I'd like to know what you do in general too. I'd also like to stop rambling incessantly."

He smiled broadly and settled his forearms on the table so that they cocooned the cup. "I'm a sports marketing executive with a firm downtown."

"I... have no idea what that is." I smiled to offset my cluelessness.

"Basically, we put businesses in contact with major sporting events and personalities. So if you're trying to plan a large-scale event and want a professional athlete there to support your brand and help gain media traction, we help make that happen."

That actually sounded fairly interesting, but saying so seemed trite. "You must get into all the cool parties," is what I said instead, which sounded cornier in reality than it had in my head.

Thankfully he just laughed. "I've been to my fair share. What about you?"

"I rarely go to parties."

He laughed again, and my face heated as I realized he'd been asking what I did for a living. I smiled in hopes of playing my idiocy off. "I'm an attorney specializing in family law."

Leaning forward, he propped his elbow on the table and rested his chin on his hand. "I bet that's a tough field to be in."

His tone was sincere, but I still found myself holding back a little. It was the first date. There was no need to go into just how emotionally draining my job could be.

"It has its ups and downs."

From there, our conversation moved into more mundane things: TV and music preferences, hobbies, interests, the usual. Not that I was an expert in "the usual." This was the first date I'd had that got this far.

I glanced down at my watch and realized we'd been talking for over an hour. It felt like time had flown, but I was also drained. Holding up my end of a getting-to-know-you conversation was exhausting, and I was powering down. Not that I hadn't enjoyed talking to him.

I could sense a potential spark of... something between us. He was articulate, funny, intelligent, and kind. Not to mention handsome as hell. Yes, Hunter was definitely someone I'd like to see more of. Later. For now, I needed to decompress.

"This has been fun," I said with a wide smile I hoped made it clear I wasn't blowing him off.

"It has," he said, returning my smile.

Since he'd been the one to approach me about going out, I figured I could at least do my part. "Would you like to do it again sometime?"

"I thought you'd never ask."

We made plans to go to dinner Friday night at a nearby seafood restaurant. He offered to pick me up, but since I'd likely be coming from the office, it made more sense to meet him there. Like the gentleman he was, he offered to walk me home, which I declined, telling him I'd get an Uber. He did walk me out to the sidewalk, though. Unfortunately, this resulted in us staring awkwardly at each other.

We both laughed as we looked at each other, and that seemed to break whatever strangeness had crept between us. He leaned in to hug me, and I took full advantage of the opportunity to feel the firm muscles beneath his clothes. When we pulled apart, he asked if I was sure I didn't want him to wait for my ride to show. Since I wasn't really leaving, I definitely didn't want him to do that.

"No. I'm actually going to run back in and use the restroom. I'll wait inside for the Uber if that makes you feel better."

Nodding, he said, "It does." He gave me a sweet smile before continuing. "I'll see you soon, then."

"Definitely."

I watched him start down the street before I made my way back inside the Bean. But instead of heading to the bathroom, I veered toward Gray's table and plopped down across from him.

He was drawing and didn't look up at me, but asked, "How'd it go?"

"Good. He's really nice."

"That's good." He sounded distracted, which made an ache lance down my sternum. Maybe it was selfish, but I was used to having all Gray's attention. It made me feel . . . icky not to have it.

"Whatcha drawing?" I asked, trying to peer at the picture.

He sat back quickly and flipped the book closed. "Just doodling."

When he moved to put the sketchpad back in his bag, I said, "Wait. You're not going to let me see it?"

"See what?"

"Tonight's drawing. Didn't you do one?"

He looked almost sheepish, which was a new look for him. "I didn't draw this one."

"Why not?" Wasn't that why he'd come? I mean, I was glad he'd been here. It was like having moral support with me. But he was supposed to get something out of these dates too. Why else would he want to sit in a coffee shop for over an hour?

He shrugged. "It just... felt wrong. I could tell this date was different from the others. I didn't want to objectify it."

I sat back in my chair, thrown a little off-kilter by what Gray had said. "It was different. It *felt* different. Like this one could actually go somewhere. But you still could've drawn it. That was the deal." I said the last part with a smile, but he didn't return it.

"That's okay. Don't worry about it."

His whole demeanor was off, and it was making my stomach feel queasy. I desperately wanted to get us onto more familiar ground.

"So what are you up to now?" It was only eight o'clock. And while I had work I could be doing, nothing was pressing. Hanging out with Gray was the more appealing option.

"Nothing. Probably just going home to watch some TV."

"Want company?"

I expected the quick acquiescence I always got, but instead, he hesitated. If my time with Hunter seemed to fly, those next few seconds with Gray nearly ground to a halt.

He looked intently at me, as if trying to read me only to find out I wasn't written in his language. But eventually, he seemed to find what he was looking for because his body relaxed.

"Yeah. Of course. We're about two episodes behind on *Top Chef*."

"Sara is totally taking it this season."

"No way. Eric has it locked."

“Keep dreaming.” I stood as he grabbed his satchel. We walked out into the night and back to his apartment where we watched *Top Chef* and made a bet to see who could better create one of the winning dishes this season. It was the perfect end to a pretty great night.

CHAPTER SEVENTEEN

ISLA

We were on our second drink each—me, white sangria with cucumbers, and Hunter, some red wine I'd never heard of.

"Are you some sort of wine connoisseur?" I spun the ice with my straw, a nervous tic I'd evidently just developed for no apparent reason. *Where the hell is Gray?* When I'd expressed my apprehension about going on a *real* date and pleaded with him to go, he'd promised me I wouldn't be in this alone—that he would come to the restaurant too. I wasn't exactly sure why that made me feel better, having him here, but I couldn't deny that it did.

"A *connoisseur*?" Hunter laughed one of those low, delicate laughs that I'd come to look forward to when we talked on the phone, mainly because I could picture the smile that went along with it—a straight row of bright white teeth, dimples bracketing his dark pink lips. "I wouldn't exactly call myself that."

"I would. I don't drink anything I can't pronounce."

"My grandparents had a wine cellar. I remember going down there as a kid because it was colder in the summer. I used to wander around the bottles, pull some out, and pretend I was old enough to drink them."

"Did you ever do it?" I leaned in, my eyes alight with the

image of a young Hunter guzzling illicit substances in his grandparents' basement.

"Nah." He sounded as disappointed as I probably looked. I'd been looking forward to a good story. "What about you? You ever do anything wild as a kid?"

"Guess it depends how you define wild." I hadn't exactly been reckless as a child, and I certainly matured exponentially after my parents' deaths, but there were times I remembered breaking the rules.

He shrugged, his smile beaming as he waited for me to answer. "Craziest thing you've ever done."

"I stole a pack of condoms from a CVS in sixth grade."

His eyebrows raised, he let out an "Okayyy."

Gray really needs to get here. Who the hell tells their hot-as-hell date who's also totally normal that she pilfered prophylactics in middle school?

"It's not how it sounds," I spit out, but there was no real denying that it was exactly how it sounded. "We'd just learned about sex in health class, and my friend Kate and I were too embarrassed to ask the teacher what a condom looked like. She'd said something about it stopping the spread of AIDS and other STDs, but I couldn't understand how."

I continued, but it was like my brain was no longer in charge of deciding what words were coming out of my mouth, like the first time I realized what I was saying was when I heard myself speak rather than when I composed the thought. I heard myself say something about condoms looking like donuts in my mind and being surprised when I found out that wasn't the truth.

Hunter's mouth stayed agape for much of my verbal purge, but it did nothing to stop my rambling. A few more comments about Kate blowing up the condom to see how big of a penis could fit in there, and I was officially finished with my story. And probably also finished with my chances with Hunter.

"Wow." He cleared his throat and shifted in his seat, though he ended up in almost the same position by the time he settled. Somehow, I'd managed to make both of us completely uncomfortable in a matter of a minute or so. "That's... definitely wild. Did you ever get caught?"

I shook my head. "Nope. Kate and I were the only ones who knew about it. Well, until now, that is."

"I feel special," he said, looking more relaxed than he had a moment ago. Hunter was picking at the crab dip when I noticed Gray sitting at a table near the bar. He gave me a nod and took a sip of his beer.

"Will you excuse me for a moment?"

"Of course," Hunter said, standing slightly when I did.

I practically ran toward the bar and the restrooms on the other side of them. With the urgency with which I excused myself, Hunter probably thought I had stomach trouble. When I was safely out of Hunter's sight, I texted Gray. About thirty seconds later, he appeared beside me.

"Where the hell have you been? I was just over there talking about AIDS."

"Wait, like the disease?"

"Yes!"

He brought a hand up to his mouth to disguise his chuckle, but I saw it anyway. And truthfully, there was no point in hiding it. I deserved to be laughed at.

"Why were you talking about AIDS?"

"Jesus, I don't know. He asked what crazy things I've done, and I told him how my friend and I stole condoms in middle school, and . . . " I threw my arms up, and he returned my frustration with that cute grin he always gave me—a combination of amusement, I think, and something I couldn't quite identify. "Just tell me what to do."

"Okay, okay. Well, for starters, do *not* talk about sexually transmitted diseases anymore. He may start to think you have one."

I let out a noise that sounded like a disgruntled toddler about to throw a tantrum. "What else?"

"Do you know about any of his hobbies or anything?"

My brain was spinning, but I remembered him saying he liked sports. "Sports, I think. He watches it and plays for some local football league or something. And he does something with sports marketing."

"Okay, good. Go back and ask him how his team's doing."

"Got it. Okay." Before returning to the table, I took a deep breath and tried to compose myself. "Wish me luck."

"I wish I could say you don't need it."

"I wish you could too." I wasn't sure why I did it—habit maybe?—but I gave Gray a quick kiss on his cheek before heading back to Hunter.

Our entrees were sitting on the table when I slid into the booth. "Looks delicious," I said. And then, "You could've started eating so it doesn't get cold."

He eyed his plate of sushi and then we both laughed.

"I swear I'm usually not this . . . dense or weird or . . . " I wasn't even sure what to call it.

"I believe you. You're a lawyer. I'm sure you're extremely intelligent."

"*Extremely* might be an exaggeration."

"Self-deprecating?"

My response was a genuine smile before I stabbed a piece of our shrimp appetizer and put it into my mouth. I'd already forgotten what Gray had said I should talk to Hunter about, which only confirmed my hypothesis that me on a date was about as effective as a turtle trying to win a race.

We talked about our plans for the next few weekends. He had his nephew's baptism and a golf outing coming up, and I had virtually nothing worth mentioning—mainly since it probably included hanging out with Gray. But the mention of golf reminded me of sports, which reminded me of what I was supposed to be talking about.

"So how's your football league going?"

He looked confused for a moment before he responded with, "Oh, that doesn't start again until the end of August."

"Oh. I thought you said you had a game recently."

"We did. It was the championship game, but we lost."

Fucking Grayson. "Oh. Sorry."

"Nothing to be sorry about," he said, and then the two of us sat in silence while we ate.

"Good," Hunter said, pointing to his sushi. He hadn't bothered to finish chewing, but somehow his comment didn't come out as impolite. "You want to try some?"

I definitely did not want to try some, because the idea of eating raw fish was about as appealing as licking a stranger's sock after a midday run, but again my mouth answered before my brain could formulate its reply.

"Sure."

I watched as Hunter cut a bite of the seaweed, rice, and fish combination and then brought it to my mouth. I could do this. I'd pretend it was medicine or a shot of cheap tequila and down it before my tongue could evaluate the flavors. Then I'd chase it with my sangria and hope for the best.

The moment it touched my tongue, I almost gagged, but somehow I managed to force it down. It wasn't the worst thing I'd tasted, but it wasn't the best either. My sangria tasted better than ever. I wondered if I tried the sushi again if I could develop a taste for it.

Sushi always seemed so sexy to me. It could only be enjoyed by the cultured and well-traveled, a culinary delicacy to be experienced by the few that could appreciate the finer things in life.

Of course I knew none of that was true, but I couldn't help but feel that I was left out of some elite club of sushi-eating, world-traveling wine connoisseurs. Which was why I'd stayed in my wheelhouse and ordered sangria and some sort of chicken stir-fry dish. I found myself wondering what Gray had ordered, and though I didn't know for sure that he wasn't fond of sushi, something told me—or maybe I just blindly hoped—that he didn't.

Hunter looked at me expectantly. "What do you think?"

"Spicy." I could feel the heat as soon as I put it in my mouth, but it was gradually becoming more intense. I took another drink.

"The alcohol and water probably make it spicier," Hunter said. "I should've warned you."

"Will you excuse me for a minute?" I said, not even waiting for an answer before I slid out of the booth. My body was heading toward Gray's table before my mind even knew I wanted to go there.

GRAYSON

Isla hadn't even been gone ten minutes before I saw her bolt out of the booth and speedwalk toward me.

"What is this?" she asked, pointing to my glass.

"Sprite." She was already drinking it before I answered.

"The carbonation wasn't helpful, but I think it got the taste out."

"What are you doing?"

"Hunter made me try sushi."

I raised an eyebrow. "He *made* you?"

"More like peer pressured me into it."

"Do I need to give him a lesson on bullying?" We both laughed, and then she grabbed my arm, pulling me away from the table and toward the bar, effectively out of Hunter's sight if he happened to turn around.

"I can't do this."

I noticed her looking everywhere but at me, and I put my hands on either side of her face to focus her eyes on mine. "Look at me."

"I'm basically a cacophony of all the horrible dates I've been on. It's like I took a page from each of them and created my own book."

That made me laugh harder, but I stopped quickly when I saw how upset she seemed. "Listen to me. You are *not* like any of the dates you've been on. I've seen those jokers, and you're the furthest thing from that."

Her eyes met mine, and the crazed look in them seemed to evaporate some.

"Really?"

"Really," I assured her. "You're smart and funny and

irresistibly beautiful. Any guy would be lucky to have you."

"I don't feel any of those things right now."

Her comment caused an emptiness to form in my chest, like it was a balloon that had the air let out without warning. How could she not see what I did? What I knew Hunter and every other guy in his right mind probably saw? I wanted to kiss the stupid out of her, make her see what I saw.

"Then you're also crazy," I said.

Her mouth turned up into a hesitant smile, like whatever anxiety she felt was preventing her from accepting it completely. She was quiet when she spoke again. "I asked him about football, but the season ended already, and then I pretended I liked sushi, but it was too spicy. And gross. So gross."

"It really is," I said.

She inhaled deeply and then sighed, bringing her eyes down to the floor as she exhaled.

"Look, just go back there and be yourself. Forget about trying to match your interests with his or pretending you like things you don't. I like you for you." It felt good to say the words aloud, even though the reason for them wasn't what I wished it was. "Hunter will too."

"You think so?"

I shrugged. "How could he not?"

She took another deep breath before heading back to the table, and I wondered if that would be the last time she came over. Either my advice would work, or she'd be back a few minutes later with another story about her botched date. And if I were being honest, I wasn't sure which I preferred.

I quickly sent her a text that said *You got this* and felt unexpected relief when she noticed it on her Apple Watch and smiled. There was a visible change in her over the rest of the date. She laughed casually, seemed genuinely interested in whatever they were talking about, and leaned in as they slowly shared a piece of chocolate cake. When Hunter finished signing the bill, he got up and headed to the restroom.

It was strange watching him, knowing who he was without him knowing me. And what was more, I knew Isla on a level he didn't—not only just a sexual one, but a personal one too, I realized. Somehow being a sex coach brought people closer together than I'd expected.

Once Hunter was gone, I wanted to text Isla to check in, but something stopped me. She didn't need me interfering with whatever was going on between them. I'd done my part, and I didn't want to overstay my welcome because suddenly my presence here made me feel like an intruder.

I closed out my tab as well and headed toward the exit only a few paces behind them. But somehow I couldn't bring myself to leave, so I waited in the vestibule on a bench while Hunter walked her out to his car, which was parked about halfway down the block.

They held hands as they strode down the sidewalk, each of them taking turns looking at the other as they spoke. Nothing seemed rushed about the moment, and it occurred to me how romantic all this should seem—the dim sky that was lit only by the half-moon, the mystery of their discussion and the sound of their voices, how happy they both looked.

I tried to be happy too, for Isla, because this was what she wanted, what I'd helped her prepare for. But the only thing I could seem to be happy about was that there was a panel of glass separating me from them when they leaned in to kiss. It made me feel like I was watching all this play out in a movie instead of real life. Too bad that wasn't the truth.

CHAPTER EIGHTEEN

GRAYSON

As I turned down my old street thirty minutes outside of New York, I wondered what crack I must've smoked that made me think it was a good idea to come back here. I should've taken Miranda up on her offer to ship my grandfather's gold watch. I couldn't even believe I'd left it to begin with. But I'd been so angry, and my need to get the hell out of there had been so urgent, that I hadn't remembered to take the family heirloom.

It wasn't until Miranda had thoroughly cleaned out the top of my closet that she'd found the watch in a box on the top shelf and had called me. It was the second time in a month that I'd had to talk to her and, in my opinion, two times too many.

Shutting off the ignition, I took a deep breath and looked down the street. Miranda's Jeep was in the driveway, the paint of the bumper still chipped from when she'd backed into my car one Saturday morning. Our front lawn—Miranda's front lawn—still sprouted the crabgrass I could never get rid of.

As I exited my car, Mr. Bristol, a retired man who'd always been friendly to us, was mowing his lawn. He brought up a hand to wave to me like he'd done hundreds of times before. It wasn't until I waved back that it seemed to occur to him that my presence there was at all out of the ordinary. His jovial expression shifted to one of confusion, and he returned his attention back to the lawn.

It took Miranda only a few moments to answer the door, and I wasn't sure how to react when she opened it. Both of us stared silently for a moment before one of us felt the need to fill the awkward silence with awkward conversation. That person was unfortunately me.

"Thanks for letting me come. I won't stay long. I just wanna take one more look around to make sure I didn't leave anything else, and then I'll be out of your way."

"No rush." She stepped out of the doorway so I could enter, and the gesture struck me as strange even though it shouldn't have. "Coffee?" she asked, pointing over her shoulder toward the kitchen. "I just started a pot."

"I'm good," I said, already heading up the stairs, but my gait slowed when I realized I was in no real hurry to enter the master bedroom. Turning around, I said, "You know what? I'll take you up on that coffee. It's been a long day."

I followed her back down the stairs, wondering when I'd get the nerve to enter the bedroom—the bedroom that used to be ours but was now hers and Dennis's. Even *thinking* about what happened in that room had me shuddering.

She handed me a cup of coffee in a mug I'd never seen before and stirred in the cream and sugar like she'd done for years before work.

"Thanks."

"You look good."

"Thanks," I said again, not wanting to return the comment. I wasn't even sure if it was a compliment. Did she mean I looked *good*? Or looked good for someone who fled the only place and people he'd ever known after his wife cheated on him with his best friend?

"The place looks different." I motioned to some of the furniture—clean, modern lines and light-cream sofas that looked so pristine, they belonged in a brochure for some luxurious resort where twenty-somethings with trust funds went to honeymoon, not in a three-bedroom in Brooklyn.

"Different bad?"

"Just different," I answered, and that seemed to satisfy her, because she didn't press me further about what I meant.

"So how have you been?"

I almost laughed. "When are you gonna realize that's like literally the shittiest question you could ask me?"

"Sorry," she said, sounding sincere. She dropped her gaze to the cup between her hands, and when she brought it up again, she said, "For a lot of things."

"If one of them isn't sleeping with my best friend, you're an even bigger asshole than I thought." My words were callous, but my tone didn't match. For as heartbroken as I'd been and as betrayed as I'd felt months ago, my current life was noticeably better than my former one, and that had more to do with Isla being *in* it than Miranda being *out* of it.

"Yeah, I'm sorry for that. I don't... Things didn't work out with Dennis. He moved out a few weeks ago."

I'd wanted this day to come, wanted to hear that her life had fallen apart after she'd caused the same to happen to mine. But the words were oddly unfulfilling. I didn't feel joy or even relief. I didn't know what I felt, exactly, so I decided I just felt nothing.

I didn't care what happened in Miranda's life or what would happen because she wasn't a part of mine, and not one part of me was attracted to her anymore. Her long red hair, once a feature that'd only increased her appeal, was like a warning sign framing her freckled face. *Stop. Do not proceed. Stranger danger.*

Because truthfully, she was a stranger, and everything about right now felt strange. I stopped listening as she spoke, too much in my own head to care if she realized. I heard her say something about making a mistake and trying again, but when my eyes darted up to her, the only thing I wanted to try again was to get my grandfather's watch and get the hell out of there.

Miranda wasn't the woman I should be talking to, and I didn't want to be sitting across from her any longer than I needed to. So I went upstairs and into the master closet, grabbed the watch and a few other items I thought might give her an excuse to reach out again, and headed back toward the front door.

"Thanks for the coffee" was the only thing I said before I made my way to my car and hopefully out of her life forever.

ISLA

"I think I'll actually miss being able to see your drawings," I said, scrolling through Gray's work Instagram account on my phone and reading the comments on my dates. This wasn't the first time I'd been on there, nor was it the first time I'd read the comments, but it gave me some sort of satisfaction to know that I wasn't the only one who thought the guys—and Hunter Number One—were worthy of being immortalized on social media.

Gray was leaning against his counter with his hands on the edge of the dark granite. "I know. Me too. Mr. Thomas finally agreed to let me put some of my cartoons up there, it creates a huge following, and now we might lose it because you had to go and find some normal dude you actually like." Casting his eyes down so that they were hidden by lids and long, dark lashes women would sell their souls for, Gray began smoothing out nonexistent wrinkles on the front of his shirt.

Hunter was a possibility—albeit a good one—but I hadn't felt that undeniable connection yet. He seemed like a good guy, had a good job, a good personality, and all of that was . . . *good.* But I couldn't help but wonder when good would be great, or even good enough.

Maybe it was too much to wish for something magical, some sort of can't-live-without-you attraction, but I couldn't stop myself from hoping that my feelings for Hunter would turn into that.

I didn't need the Disney fairy tale where the hero comes and sweeps the lost, down-on-her-luck princess off her feet. I wasn't lost or down-on-my-luck, and I sure as hell wasn't a princess, but that little girl inside me wanted that feeling anyway—the one where I would know without a shadow of a doubt that this was the man I was supposed to be with.

"I don't *like him* like him." I wasn't sure what prompted me to say that, but I needed to make the distinction clear.

Gray slid his hands into his pockets. "I don't even know what that means."

I laughed, hoping Gray would too. He didn't. "Me neither. I guess . . ." *I guess I wish he were you.* I immediately wished I'd never thought it. Because until now, that realization had been an abstract concept, a feeling that I refused to give any credence to. And now I knew why. Gray's body might not be off-limits, but the man was.

I knew how much the situation with his ex had fucked him up, and I knew—because he'd told me more than once—that he could never put himself out there like that again. I wasn't in a place to convince him otherwise, nor did I want to do that to him. If Gray had feelings for me, he'd tell me—even if sometimes he looked at me a little longer than necessary and smiled at me in a sweet way that made me want to believe his feelings ran more deeply.

"I guess I just wish I knew he liked me like I like him. It would make it easier for me to tell him how I feel. It's like I can't let myself acknowledge my feelings completely until I know my feelings will be reciprocated." I knew how insecure the admission made me sound, but I couldn't find it in myself to care.

A small smile played on Gray's lips, but it didn't have the chance to fully form before he spoke again. "I'm sure he likes you." This time the smile found its way over his whole face, making the creases near his eyes more defined and the dimples beneath his sandy stubble more pronounced. "How could he not?"

I'd been standing back a few feet from him, my back pressing against the island in the middle of his kitchen, but I suddenly felt the need to step closer to him, like the decreased physical distance might somehow bring us closer emotionally too. He looked incredibly attractive, his chest and arms filling his untucked button-down perfectly.

Wrapping my arms around his neck, I said, "I *am* pretty likable."

Gray brought his hands up to my hips, but they felt unsettled there, like he wasn't sure where exactly they belonged. I wanted to tell him they belonged everywhere—in my hair, on my nipples, the inside of my thighs, anywhere he wanted to put them. But like always, I couldn't find the right words, so I hoped my actions might speak for me. Gray's touch was gentle as I brought my lips to his, and for a brief, wonderful moment, he kissed me as passionately as I kissed him.

Until he didn't.

All movement stopped between us as I sensed our exchange coming to an end. When Gray guided my hips away from him, I knew that truth for certain. He dropped his hands, and his gaze followed.

Unwilling to let him look away from me, I brought his chin up enough to make eye contact with him.

"What's wrong?"

"I think we should stop this."

"Stop what?" I asked, needing him to clarify something that didn't necessitate clarification. I knew exactly what he was referring to, and I had no idea why I'd wanted to hear him explain further.

"Having sex. Seeing each other. Whatever this is." He gestured between us, and his voice was so calm, his expression so stoic, that I wondered if he'd practiced the lines before so it would come across the way he wanted it to: simple, casual, inevitable. And in truth, it was. This moment was always going to happen. I just found myself wishing it didn't have to. "You like this guy, and I'm sure he likes you. It could be something even if it isn't anything yet." He rubbed a hand over his mouth like he was debating whether to continue. After a few seconds, he said, "You deserve to give it a shot—both of you—without any interference from me."

"You aren't interfering."

"Does he know you're sleeping with me?"

Surprised at the question, I jerked my head back. "He doesn't know I'm *not* sleeping with you. We haven't talked about seeing other people." I knew the argument was about as strong as a straw house, and it wouldn't stand for very long, but I couldn't seem to come up with anything better.

The thought of not sleeping with Gray any longer had me more disappointed than I cared to admit, even internally. Until now, I'd never thought our relationship had been about more than just sex, but now, suddenly the loss of it felt like a gigantic hole in the pit of my stomach.

"But I get what you're saying. It complicates things."

"Right," he said. "I've had enough of complicated."

It occurred to me that he was probably referring to his divorce, but I didn't feel the need to acknowledge it aloud. And ultimately, if Hunter and I took things further—which was a definite possibility—things would only get messier for everyone involved. It was better if Gray and I cut ties now.

"Okay then," I said, putting on my best I'm-totally-okay-with-this face and extending a hand to him because I felt like some sort of physical contact was in order, but a hug seemed too intimate. "Friends?"

"Friends," he repeated.

He took my hand in his, and I wondered if this might be the last time we touched, because I had no idea how I could be friends with Grayson Hawkins.

CHAPTER NINETEEN

GRAYSON

It was harder than I'd expected, being friends with Isla. Maybe because we'd never actually been friends to begin with. We'd just been two strangers in a coffeehouse, flirting subtly until it wasn't so subtle. Then we'd been sexual partners before we'd ever really gotten a chance to become friends. Which was odd because when we weren't having sex, we had good conversation and had similar interests. Wasn't that what friends did? We could make each other laugh as easily as we could make each other come. Though unfortunately there wouldn't be any more of the latter.

After I suggested an end to our physical relationship, Isla and I gave our friendship the old college try. We really did. We'd gone out to the movies once—my pick—and Isla hadn't seemed thrilled with it. And then another time this past week, because I'd felt bad about the movie thing, I'd suggested we go to an outdoor food fair in the city.

The weather was gorgeous, the food and beer were delicious, and the atmosphere relaxed and upbeat. But still, we couldn't seem to find our groove, despite both of us clearly trying. It was like the lack of sex had created an empty place in our relationship so cavernous that we couldn't help but hear its echo.

Even though what we had was ostensibly based on sex, at some point a seed had been planted inside me that said we could be more than that. But before I'd given it a chance to grow, to see what it might become, I'd gone and killed it. Buried it somewhere so deep that it could never be brought to light. And now, here we were, sitting on Isla's couch, bottles of beer in hand, struggling to make conversation.

Why is this so fucking weird?

I wondered if Isla felt it too, but I didn't want to ask. I wasn't sure if it was because I was more worried she felt the same way I did, or worried that nothing seemed out of the ordinary to her and all this tension was simply a manifestation of my fucked-up mind. Which would mean my instincts had been all wrong and Isla didn't have feelings for me beyond sexual ones. And that was some shit I didn't want to think about right now. Or ever actually.

Isla scrolled through her phone, seemingly excited to show me some video of a guy who appeared to be having an actual conversation with the baby next to him. She laughed hysterically while I struggled to fake a smile.

"Hunter sent me this the other day. I keep watching it over and over. Never gets old."

Nope, definitely not feeling the same thing I am right now.

"So things with Hunter are going well? Progressing?" My formal questions sounded more like a therapist's than a friend's, and I hoped she didn't pick up on my lack of enthusiasm for her new relationship.

"I guess so." She sounded chipper, though she didn't elaborate.

I nodded, wondering if the silence would cause her to share any more. Did her hesitance to tell me anything else mean they hadn't slept together? Or did it mean they had? None of this should even matter to me, but as I watched Isla take another sip of her beer, it was *all* that seemed to matter. Those lips now spoke about another guy when they should be used to kiss me.

But I could never actually tell her that. So instead I said, "How's the sex?"

Her eyes widened at the question, and I could only guess it was because she wasn't expecting me to ask it. "I'm not sure." She almost laughed but pressed her lips together in an obvious attempt to stop it from escaping.

I'd once asked her if she realized she did that when she was embarrassed, and she said she did and she'd tried more than once to stop but couldn't. I'd told her it was a good thing she couldn't do it because it was adorable and sweet and sexy as hell. It now occurred to me that those weren't compliments you give some rando you're sleeping with, and I wondered if she'd realized that then.

"We haven't exactly had sex yet."

"Exactly?" *Why do you ask questions you don't want the answer to?*

"I mean we've fooled around a bit, but we haven't gone all the way. I have no idea why, though." She did that thing with her lips again. "Hunter's good-looking and a good kisser, so he's probably good in bed."

"Probably," I agreed. *When the hell did I become her gay best friend who is so not gay?*

"What do you think?" she asked expectantly. "Should I do it?"

No! I wanted to scream at her that she should absolutely not fuck this douche. Okay, Hunter might not be a douche, but he was a douche in my mind because he had the woman I wanted—the woman I had, or maybe could've had if I had the balls to tell her what I thought about her. What I *felt*.

But I didn't deserve her, and she certainly didn't deserve me. She deserved a normal guy who wasn't damaged and jaded beyond repair. A guy exactly like Hunter.

"Definitely." I nodded enthusiastically for effect and hoped it wasn't too over the top. "You should totally have sex with him. If you want to, I mean. Wasn't that what we were practicing all that time for?" I said. But what I thought was, *I can't be friends with her anymore.*

And just like that, I somehow became a pussy and a dick at exactly the same time.

CHAPTER TWENTY

ISLA

"This is nice," I said, settling myself closer to Hunter because I enjoyed the feeling of my head nestling against his warm body, feeling the hard muscles of his chest as I listened to his heartbeat. He smelled spicy and fresh as I inhaled deeply. And I felt like a teenage girl on prom night about to lose her virginity to the captain of the football team.

This was it. I could feel it.

Well, actually I'd already felt *it* plenty of times through my pants when I straddled him during our intense make-out sessions. I just hadn't felt him inside me yet, and the anticipation was killing me.

"It is." He grabbed the remote from beside him and clicked off the TV.

"What'd you do that for?" My voice was intentionally whiny.

Tossing the remote down again so he could wrap a hand around me, he said, "Because I don't want anything to distract me from you tonight."

The weight of his body felt perfect on mine. Just enough to apply pressure where I needed it without completely bearing down on me. I moaned when his tongue entered my mouth and he began to move over me.

We'd done this so many times before—the slow grind against each other. But I knew Hunter wanted more. Any guy would. But he was taking his time, waiting until I gave him the green light to round third and slide into home. Yup, I definitely felt like a teenager.

My clothes came off before his and fell in a discarded heap next to Hunter's couch. His followed a bit later, as I was sure he hoped we were nearing the overdue consummation of our relationship.

It was a solid strategy, I'd give him that. And seeing him in all his naked glory as he stood above me had me wondering why I hadn't done this earlier. Hunter was hot and sweet and perfect in all the ways that mattered.

Except... it didn't *quite* feel like it mattered the way it should. This didn't *feel* the way it should. And I knew that because I'd experienced how it *should* feel, even though I hadn't realized it at the time.

As Hunter kissed me and touched me, all I could think about was how I wished it was someone else's hands and tongue on me.

I wished he was Gray.

So as turned on as I was as he put a condom on and lined himself up to me, I couldn't go through with it.

"I can't," was all I said, and Hunter immediately backed off, gave me space. It only made me feel worse. Why did he have to be such a fucking nice guy?

"Sorry. Are you okay? Did I do something?"

"No." I shook my head quickly, needing him to know he wasn't to blame for what was probably going to be the worst case of blue balls he'd ever experienced. "No, it's not you, it's me."

He was seated next to me and, obviously sensing the gravity of my tone, had already started grabbing his clothes from the floor and the arm of the couch.

"You know that's like the worst line ever, right?" He laughed as he said it, but the disappointment on his face betrayed his real feelings.

He was more than just sexually frustrated. He was probably frustrated period, because we had something good, or *could've* had something good if I didn't have feelings for some guy who was probably incapable of having those sorts of feelings for any other woman ever again.

I almost laughed too because Gray was right: I really knew how to pick 'em. I went out with a bunch of losers, accidentally had a date with a woman, and then let go of a perfectly available, sweet guy because the only guy I'd ever truly fallen for was completely out of reach.

"It really is me," I assured him, though I knew the words did nothing to help the situation.

So I simply got dressed and headed to the door without saying anything else. I chanced one more look over my shoulder before I left.

He was still on the couch, his clothes in his hands, but he hadn't put any of them on yet. He looked like a dog who'd just been put back in his cage at a shelter after he thought he might get adopted by this nice woman who'd just spent time playing with him.

Sorry, buddy.

He lifted a hand in goodbye before letting it fall back onto his thigh. I assumed as soon as I left, it would find its way to his cock, which I noticed was still incredibly hard beneath the condom. I was a real fucking asshole sometimes.

♦♦♦♦

The drive home was filled with so many thoughts and emotions that I couldn't make sense of any of them, let alone all of them. What the hell was I supposed to do with this? I couldn't tell Gray what I felt because he wasn't in a place to want any type of relationship.

But stronger than that knowledge was the knowledge that I couldn't just let this go. Whatever we had was something. Or maybe I just hoped it would be. But I didn't think he'd give it a chance. And it was selfish of me to ask him to.

So I fought the urge to go to his house on the way home. I didn't call him. And I didn't even text him. The restraint was both satisfying and completely dejecting all at once. When I got into bed, I convinced myself that with time I could get over him. That I'd be able to move on eventually. But my lack of sleep told me differently.

During the night, I drifted in and out of consciousness, never sleeping long enough to feel at all rested. I dreamed I was in Gray's house, yelling at him as he sat on the couch, but he couldn't hear me. I dreamed Gray and I were having sex, and I was so close to coming, but something prevented me from doing so. I woke up a sweaty mess, tangled in sheets and blankets as I tried to dissect my dreams for a meaning I already knew.

I wanted Gray. I just didn't think he wanted me back.

But there was this little spark of hope inside me that said otherwise. Maybe he'd only wanted a friendship with me wasn't because it wasn't fair to Hunter and me. Maybe it was because of something more—something neither of us wanted to admit.

I texted him.

You awake?

It was after four in the morning, and I was pretty sure of the answer.

When there was no response, I tried my best to get some rest but had little success, which was not surprising. Despite my lack of sleep, I found myself wishing for morning as if the light of day might bring clarity to where I was supposed to go from here.

When the sun finally rose a little while later, I pulled one of the pillows against me, hugging it like I would Gray if he were here. It smelled like him. I'd noticed it last night, but I hadn't wanted to use it all up. As if every inhale might diminish its potency. It might be all I had left of Gray.

But why was that? I could easily understand why he wouldn't want to continue a sexual relationship when I was hoping to become intimate with someone else. But why did I have to lose his friendship too?

And that was when it hit me. Maybe, all this time, I'd had more of Gray than I'd thought. He'd told me—and I'd believed him—that he didn't want to get emotionally involved with anyone again. That anything beyond sex was too much for him.

But maybe it wasn't too much for him anymore.

The thought echoed inside my brain before I'd realized its implication. *But maybe it wasn't too much for him anymore,* I thought again. Maybe the reason Gray wanted to create distance between us was because he was scared of getting too close, scared I'd hurt him like Miranda did.

I wouldn't.

But of course he didn't know that, and I had no way of convincing him of that, except to try. I texted him again that I needed to talk, and when he asked what about, I stupidly answered that I needed to talk about what happened last night with Hunter. I shouldn't have been surprised when he declined, simply wishing the both of us luck.

The next day I tried calling. I even left a voicemail saying I couldn't go through with sleeping with Hunter, but since he once warned me never to leave a voicemail because he rarely ever listened to them, I was sure he didn't even play it.

I texted him yet again, asking to get together, but he just told me he'd been busy and he didn't know when he might have time.

All of it was stupid. Presumptuous really, when I thought about it. He was my sex coach, and I was his student. But...

But there was a chance that I was wrong. Maybe we'd always been more than that and had simply refused to acknowledge it. Maybe I'd been looking for something I'd had the whole time.

Maybe I had to do more than just text and call him. Maybe I had to think bigger.

CHAPTER TWENTY-ONE

GRAYSON

I sat at my desk editing pictures on my computer. Well, I was *supposed* to be editing pictures. Mostly I was aimlessly clicking through image after image so they formed almost a kaleidoscope of color that took on no particular form.

Sighing heavily, I sat up and rubbed my eyes. When I'd come to this town, I was trying to escape the very feeling currently thrumming through my system. It stemmed from loneliness, yet it was more than that. There was loss here now.

My life had a duller quality because I'd lost something I'd never have again. Granted, in both instances I'd *chosen*. I'd chosen to leave my marriage—though there hadn't been much left to save of that—and I'd chosen to cut ties with Isla, which had been a matter of self-preservation.

But I had to question what I was preserving. It certainly wasn't my happiness, because I was as miserable as I'd ever been. Maybe we could've made a friendship work. Maybe having her in my life in that capacity would be better than not having her there at all.

I didn't think so, though. Watching her be happy with someone else was a fate worse than being perennially alone. Just because I wasn't right for her didn't mean I wanted to watch her with someone who was.

Groaning, I stood and grabbed my coffee mug. As I stretched, Dax appeared beside my desk.

"Hey, man. Anything new on Instagram?"

My eyes narrowed as I looked at him. It was an odd question. What the hell would be new on Instagram? I hadn't posted on there in over a week, unable to even log in and confront the origin of a friendship that no longer was.

"Not that I know of," I replied as I moved around him and started toward the break room.

He walked with me, his shoulder lightly bumping mine as we made our way down the tight aisle.

"You should check. Just in case."

"In case what?" I turned into the break room and went straight for the Keurig, popping a K-cup in and putting my mug in place to catch the elixir that would allow me to survive this day. Or at least this conversation.

He flustered for a second, his eyes widening and his mouth working silently with words he hadn't yet chosen to voice. "Oh, uh, I don't know. Maybe we got some new comments on one of your drawings or something."

"Did you see any comments?"

"No."

"Then why would you think there are any?"

Movement caught the corner of my eye, and I turned to see Curtis, Lynda, and Jess come in and settle around the table.

Dax gave them a quick glance that looked beseeching before he focused back on me. "Why do *you* think there aren't any?"

"Because I have no reason to think there are."

"You should check," Jess contributed. "Things are in

a constant state of flux. Nothing is stagnant. Time passes, people change, pictures appear. Good pictures. Pictures you should totally look at."

"I'll keep that in mind," was all I could say without insulting them all. I grabbed my mug and hightailed it out of the room.

Once I settled back at my desk, I vowed to get some work done. There was a feature going out that needed a photo to accompany it, and though I'd taken a ton, none jumped out at me as being "the one." But after a little bit of playing around with the contrast and aspect ratio, I had one I thought would work. I was changing the brightness when I heard a throat clear.

"That's pretty. Is it going up on social media?" asked Curtis, leaning in like the answer to his question would reveal important national secrets.

"No," I replied, dragging out the vowel. "It's going into the next issue."

"Oh. You should put it on social media too. Specifically Instagram. They like all that artsy crap on there, don't they?"

I resisted the urge to call him out for labeling my photo 'artsy crap,' but it was difficult.

"Did you need something?" I asked instead.

"Me? No, no, don't need anything. Just checking in."

"Why?" In all the time I'd worked here, Curtis had never felt the need to "check in" with me before today.

"It's, um, it's…just a new thing I'm doing. Taking an interest in others."

"How's that working for you?"

"Not so great. It's kind of exhausting."

I nodded like he was making sense and then turned back to my computer.

"So, just to be clear, you're not going to check Instagram?"

Part of me wanted to give in, but the more stubborn part didn't because of how annoying and vague everyone was being.

"Nope."

"Oh. Okay," Curtis said before hustling away.

Out of the corner of my eye, I saw all of them convene and whisper at Jess's desk. Something was obviously up, and while I was morbidly curious at what they were trying to get me to see, fucking with them was the most fun I'd had in weeks. I pretended to be busy at my desk while keeping a surreptitious eye on them.

"I've had enough of this shit," Lynda yelled before storming away from the group and heading right for me.

I kept working, intrigued by the "shit" she'd had enough of but wanting to play it cool.

When she reached me, she crossed her arms over her chest and stared at me.

"Can I help you with something?" I asked, blasé about her presence as I played around with a picture on my computer.

"Go on Instagram. Right. Now."

"Hmm, I'm a little busy right now. Maybe later."

"Grayson."

When she didn't continue, I chanced a glance up at her.

"Do it now." She was practically snarling at me.

"I'm sure I'll get to it—"

The rest of my words were cut off by her grabbing my keyboard, yanking its cords free of my monitor, and flinging it like a Frisbee across our office.

I worked my lips for a second before I pointed to where my keyboard had landed. "You know I don't actually need that to edit my pictures, right?"

"The monitor is next," she warned.

"What's going on out here?" I heard Mr. Thomas ask, though I didn't dare look away from Lynda. "Lynda, did you throw a keyboard across the room?"

Also unwilling to break eye contact, Lynda replied with a curt, "Yup. And heads are going to start rolling in a minute if this dickhead doesn't get his stupid ass on Instagram."

"I'm definitely not posting pictures of my ass on Instagram," I retorted, because I'd evidently sunken to her pre-teen level.

She rested her hands on my desk and leaned into my space, which caused me to shrink back into my chair. Her whole demeanor was more than a little frightening.

"Grayson," she said, her voice low and menacing. "I've always almost liked you. So I'm going to give you one more warning before I roll you like a dumpster diver. Get on your phone and log on to Instagram. Now."

I wasn't sure what her words even meant exactly, but I knew she meant them all the same.

"Lynda, you can't threaten the staff. It's not—"

"Not now, Tommy. I have a message to send."

I heard Mr. Thomas sputter at her interruption and odd abbreviation of his last name, but I was too busy fishing my phone out of my pocket to look over at him.

"Christ, everyone here is fucking nuts, I swear. Fine, I'm on Instagram." I held my phone out so she could see the screen. "Happy now?"

"Go to our page."

After rolling my eyes, I clicked on our profile and watched it load. I was so busy being petulant, it took me a moment to notice that the most recent illustration wasn't one I'd posted.

I clicked on it and was taken aback by how horrible it was. Had a toddler taken control of our page?

But looking closer, I was able to see it for what it was.

It was two people—both fairly androgynous but for one having long hair—smiling at each other. Around them were a variety of items: a coffee cup—I think—a feather, handcuffs, a pencil and paper, and a few other things I was hard-pressed to decipher because the drawing was *that* bad. But between them was a heart, and it was the only part of the picture that was colored in.

"You guys are into some weird shit," Lynda said as she looked over my shoulder. "I approve."

Ignoring her, I looked down at the caption.

Sometimes we're so close to something, we don't see it for what it really is. All the things we shared, I wasn't just sharing them with my sexpert. I was sharing them with the boyfriend I didn't even realize I had until you were gone. But now that I finally see the truth, I know without a doubt that no one else will ever mean as much to me as you do.

Grayson, I want you to keep drawing me failing at life so we can laugh about it on your couch. I want to do all the things that best friends who fall in love do. I don't even know what those things are, but I'm sure we'll figure it out. As long as you're with me, I'll always figure it out. Please tell me I didn't ruin it before it even truly started.

XOXO, Isla

I reread the caption again, and then a third time.

"You're hesitating. Why is he hesitating?" Lynda asked.

I looked up and saw the rest of them crowded around my desk.

"Is he crying?" Jess asked.

"Not yet, but it looks like he's close," Lynda added.

"What's going on?" Mr. Thomas asked.

He was immediately shushed by Dax, who announced that we were "having a moment."

"This is spanning longer than a moment," Curtis said. "Why isn't he saying anything?"

"Because he's emotionally disabled, like all men. Fucking worthless." Lynda huffed as she finished speaking, like she was indignant on Isla's behalf.

"Give him a minute. He's processing." Jess's voice sounded like she was talking about a dog who was too dumb to learn how to sit.

Lynda scoffed. "For fuck's sake, stop being so understanding. It's nauseating."

"Don't get mad at me just because I'm a people person and you're a cynical shrew."

"You know what, Jessicunt? You're lucky I can't kill people with my mind, because you'd be fucked."

"Whatever, Lyndorrhea. You don't scare—"

"Can you both shut the fuck up for a second?" I finally said. "And go away. I have a phone call to make."

Jess immediately lost all traces of agitation and looked at me as if I was recreating her favorite rom-com moment. "Are you going to call Isla? Because she seemed really nice when she emailed and asked us to post her picture."

"Totally," Dax agreed. "I mean, her drawing skills suck, but it's the thought that counts and all that. Right?"

There were murmurs of agreement from around me, but

I ignored them in favor of selecting Isla's name on my phone as I stood to start gathering my things.

"Hello?" came the tentative voice on the other end of the line.

I stopped what I was doing and let those two syllables wash over me.

"Hey." Silence filled the connection between us for a second before I was able to push more words out of my mouth. "I saw your picture."

"Would you believe that was my fifth draft? I'd almost forgotten what a horrible artist I am."

I chuckled into the line. "Yeah, it was pretty terrible."

"Ah, well, can't be good at everything."

"No, that would be unfair to the rest of us." It was her turn to laugh, and I waited until it was quiet again before I continued. "The caption was pretty great, though."

I heard her take a deep breath. "It was maybe a little sappy." Her tone made it clear she was teasing, but there was uncertainty laced into the words.

"Maybe a tad. That's what made it perfect, though."

"Perfectly sappy?"

"Perfectly everything."

She sniffled. "Gray, I'm so sorry. I didn't—"

"Can we not do this over the phone? Christ, that was rude. I'm sorry to interrupt, but can I come see you? I just . . . I *need* to see you."

I needed her like I needed my next breath would've been a more honest statement, but I didn't want to completely overplay my hand. Every moment we'd been apart for the last few weeks had been gut-wrenching, and there was no lifting that burden until I could see her face and know it was real.

I wasn't naïve to think my own hang-ups had simply disappeared, but wasn't this the chance I'd wanted? The chance that had caused me to pull away from her because I thought I had no shot at getting it? I'd be a fucking moron to let it—let *her*—slip through my fingers.

It sounded like she released a sigh into the phone. "Yeah, I need to see you too."

I grabbed my bag and maneuvered around my gawking coworkers and headed toward the exit.

"Are you at work? I'll come to you right now," I said.

"Actually, I'm a bit closer than work."

"Great. Where are you?"

"On the sidewalk outside your office."

I stopped in my tracks. "That's... convenient." Getting moving again, I pressed the down button for the elevator.

"Yeah. The security guard in your building has been watching me for a while. Which, in his defense, makes sense since I've been here almost two hours."

"Two hours?" In my surprise, I practically yelled the words. "You've been waiting down there all that time?"

"Maybe just do what we say the first time from now on," Lynda yelled from behind me.

As the elevator slid open, I gave her a wave over my shoulder that was more of a fuck off than a goodbye, but she could take it however she wanted.

"You were really taking your time up there," Isla said. "It was making me nervous."

"Well, in about two minutes, I'll start making up for keeping you waiting." I watched the numbers tick down as the elevator descended.

"You'd better. See you soon."

And with that, the call disconnected, and I was left with my foot tapping wildly and enough hope to nearly bowl me over. Today had turned into a pretty great day.

CHAPTER TWENTY-TWO

ISLA

Waiting for Gray had been a long, painful process. His coworker Jess had been keeping me updated on his stubborn ass, which I appreciated, but it didn't help alleviate the anxiety. What if he'd seen it and still hadn't wanted to talk to me? I'd have run the risk of getting tased by his building's overzealous security guard for nothing.

But when he'd finally called, I knew everything was going to be okay. Sure, we probably had some shit to sort through, but that was fine. I'd sort through anything as long as I got him at the end of it.

It had taken me a few days to come up with the idea of drawing the picture and another couple of days to work up the nerve to reach out to his colleagues for help. They quickly agreed, but they evidently weren't the most convincing bunch. Oh well. Beggars couldn't be choosers.

As I stood there staring at the door for any sign of Gray, I let it wash over me again just how big a moron I was. The man of my dreams had literally been cuffing me to headboards and listening to me bitch about my day for weeks, and I hadn't realized he was the one. How fucking dense could a person be? My level of obtuseness would actually be awe-inspiring if it hadn't almost cost me a happy future.

Finally, I saw him push through the doors of the building and stride up to me. I hadn't thought about what I was going to say once I had him down here, and panic suddenly filled my body.

Gray walked directly into my space, cupped the back of my neck with a big, warm hand, and drew my mouth to his. I should've known my sexpert would know just what to do.

The tension I'd been holding in my body faded away as I let myself get lost in him. This. This was what coming home felt like. This was the feeling I'd only ever heard about, had been convinced I could find if I looked hard enough.

As it turned out, I hadn't had to look at all. It had been sitting across from me in a coffee shop goofing on my ridiculous dates the whole time.

It was one of those time-slowing, traffic-stopping moments that only existed in the movies but felt as though the importance of it could warp reality and make the earth revolve around us for a change. And boy, if there was ever a kiss that could cause a tear in the fabric between reality and fantasy, it was this one.

As his lips smoothly moved against mine, I realized that this was our true first kiss—the one I'd always remember. This kiss wasn't clouded by pretenses and deals. This was pure, uninhibited passion, and I was a fan in a big way.

I opened my mouth to gasp, and his tongue stole inside to tangle with mine. He tilted his head slightly, which allowed him to deepen the kiss to the point I felt I might drown. I slid my arms around him tightly, as if he was my buoy in unfamiliar, though not unwelcome, waters.

He pulled his lips from mine so he could trail kisses along my jaw, and when he reached my ear, he whispered, "I missed you." And with that, I let myself be swept away in the current that was Grayson Hawkins, confident that what we had would keep me afloat.

"I missed you too," I murmured.

He pulled back enough to look into my eyes, and I could tell from the crinkling at the corners that he was smiling. We exchanged a few more gentle but brief kisses before we parted enough to talk.

"I can't believe you came for me," he said. "I really am like Julia Roberts in *Pretty Woman*."

My laugh echoed down the street and likely garnered us more stares than our kiss had. "I can deal with being Richard Gere."

He chuckled for a beat before sobering. "I'm sorry I haven't been around. It's just... it was hard. Watching you with him. Knowing he was getting everything I wanted."

I shushed him. "I'm the one who should be sorry. I don't understand how I could've missed all these feelings. Once I recognized them for what they were, they were practically dripping from my pores. I was covered in fucking *feelings*. But I was in denial or something. It was like I'd so thoroughly convinced myself I'd never have you that I didn't even let myself see our relationship for what it was. And instead I projected all those feelings onto Hunter." I took a breath before continuing. "Which was pretty shitty all around, because I think I hurt the poor guy."

"Fuck Hunter," he practically growled, which was totally unnecessary but seriously hot as hell.

"There was absolutely no fucking of Hunter," I told him because it needed to be said. I didn't want him wondering about what had happened between us.

"Really?" He looked ridiculously pleased. It shouldn't have been so endearing.

"Really."

"So I'm still the only one who's . . . ?"

I rolled my eyes. "We've been over this. I was *not* a virgin when we met."

He scoffed. "You practically were. Like a born-again virgin."

"That's so not a thing."

"For the sake of my ego, can it be a thing?"

"I don't think your ego is lacking."

"Oh yeah? Try almost losing the girl you love to a pair of Hunters."

"A *pair* of Hunters?"

His smirk should've clued me in to the fact that I was going to be affronted by his next remark. "Yeah. Don't tell me you didn't have a *lesbihonest* moment after meeting the first Hunter."

Groaning, I smacked him on the arm. "You're the worst."

"And yet still somehow the best."

I twined my arms around his neck. "Maybe because you just said you loved me."

"Caught that, did you?"

"Most definitely. Though I'm not opposed to hearing it again."

He pushed my hair away from my face, and then he cupped my jaw. "I love you, Isla."

I gazed back at him, smiling, hoping my feelings for this man were clear. "I love you too."

"Good," he whispered before closing the short distance between us and sealing our mouths together again.

Neither of us pushed to take things further, but we remained there in our own world for too long if the loud wolf whistle was anything to judge by.

"We should maybe take this somewhere more private," he said, though he didn't make any move to step away from me.

"Yeah, that's probably a good idea."

We stood still for a second longer, as if we were worried to break the spell we were under. But we finally parted, and Gray grabbed my hand and laced our fingers.

"My place or yours?"

I thought for a second. "Your place has the sex treasure chest."

He looked over at me and gave me a smile. "I don't think we need any props today. Just you and me."

Tears pricked the backs of my eyes. I almost didn't have this man. How absolutely tragic that would've been.

I squeezed his hand and said, "Just us sounds perfect."

"My place is closer, though," he said.

"Your place it is, then."

We walked quickly, exchanging brief snippets of what had been going on in our lives since we'd last spoken. Not a second too soon, we arrived at Gray's place. I faked patience while he unlocked the door and led me upstairs to his apartment, where I had to wait again for him to unlock the door.

But once we were inside and he'd kicked the door shut, all pretense of patience was gone. We were on each other like we were attempting to establish a covalent bond.

He hoisted me up, and I wrapped my legs around him as he pressed my back against the door. I ran my hands over him like he was going to disappear if I didn't touch him everywhere.

And lucky for me, it seemed like he felt the same way. His

hands were on my breasts, my ass, my shoulder blades after he pulled my shirt over my head and held me in place with his hips. It was probably the hottest thing I'd ever experienced. I was a puddle of feelings, both physical and emotional.

My skin was hot, like a fire had been lit inside me and was making its way out through my flesh as Gray kissed me. Nothing, *nothing* had ever felt this good before. This right.

My body molded to his like it had been created to fit there—the way he cupped my lower back as it arched, how perfectly his lips melted against the sensitive place between my collarbone and my neck, how delicious his cock felt between my legs.

All of it made me wonder why I'd ever thought this wasn't what I was supposed to have, wasn't *who* I was supposed to be with. Because without a doubt, I was drunk on Grayson Hawkins, and I never wanted to sober up.

At some point, he must've put me down, but I was too wrapped up in the moment to take notice of how our clothes ended up on the floor below us. All I could focus on was his coarse facial hair brushing over my chest on his way lower.

He dipped down, both hands on either of my thighs as he knelt in front of me. Still against the door, I wondered how many of his neighbors could hear me moaning, yelling his name in between choppy breaths as he licked and sucked me so fucking good I wondered if Gray might drown down there.

He brought his face back up to mine before I could come, dragging his lips over my torso as he wet it with his tongue. With his solid hands, Gray held me steady, but I still wondered if I might collapse. Was it possible to pass out from pleasure? Because someone might need to call an ambulance once Gray got done with me. It'd been weeks since I'd felt him inside me, but it seemed longer. Needing to remember the feel of him, I begged him to fuck me.

He ground his hips against me, driving me up off the ground as he lubricated himself on my pussy without pressing into it.

"I'm not gonna fuck you," he said, and I swear I could've started crying. But when he followed it with, "I'm gonna make love to you," I actually shed a few tears.

I don't think Gray noticed, though I wouldn't have cared if he had. But I knew the implications of it. This man was it for me. He was the one who'd wake me up with a kiss to the forehead before work and the one who'd make me forget about a bad day with a glass of wine and a dumb joke.

I was just glad I was it for him too.

GRAYSON

I'd said I was going to make love to Isla, but when our bodies finally connected fully, I don't know that either of us could've called it "making love."

"I don't know if I can be gentle," I said, my cock surrounding itself with the walls of her pussy as I resisted the urge to slam into her. This was the first time we'd had sex as a couple, and I wanted it to be special, memorable in a way that didn't involve being screwed into oblivion against an apartment door.

Isla looked up at me, her hand grabbing hold of my face as she spoke. "You have the rest of your life to be gentle."

I smiled at the thought.

Then her fingers found my back, nails digging into my skin in a way that would cause marks for days. All of it was rougher than I'd anticipated, harder and faster, probably because both of us felt the distance of the past few weeks and were making up for our mistakes.

Neither of us spoke anymore. Our eyes said more than any words could have, and my gaze didn't leave her.

We each took as much as we gave, and I found myself wondering if I'd ever be able to come up for air. I wondered if I'd ever *want* to. I could drown in this. In *us*. Because in some crazy twist of fate, my crumbling, fragmented semblance of a life had somehow led me to the best thing that could have ever happened to it.

I buried myself in her, filling her with short, staggered thrusts that were more frantic than rhythmic. I held on to the sound and the sight of Isla when she finally came, like if I didn't pay attention, the moment might slip from me without my being able to fully experience it. Her mouth opened, and a few little whines escaped it. Her eyes closed, and her skin flushed with the heat of all of it.

I wanted to put my lips on her, kiss the pink parts of her as she rode out the last waves of her orgasm. But my own release had been creeping up on me like a shadow I couldn't outrun any longer. So I finally stopped trying. I let it envelop me completely, like a blanket that wrapped both of us up from the inside out until we were alone in our cocoon.

Once both of us had lost all control, I slowed down to kiss her. Then I took both her hands in one of mine and pinned them above her head, my lips finally finding all the places I wanted to taste when she came.

She gripped my hips harder with her thighs in response, like if she didn't hold on tight she might lose me completely. I wanted to tell her she'd never lose me. That we could do this over and over until both of us tired of the other. And then we could do it again. Because, as Isla said, we had the rest of our lives.

And the rest of our lives sounded pretty damn good.

ALSO AVAILABLE FROM
WATERHOUSE PRESS

Keep reading for an excerpt!

EXCERPT FROM
MISADVENTURES WITH A MASTER

KATHERINE

I've been to Crave a dozen times, but I've never been as overwhelmed as I am right now. I've seen him here before, but I've always avoided his gaze. I certainly never knew his name. Now that I do, it suits him. Demitri Nicoloff is enormous. His presence... everything about him. He's one of the most intimidating people I've ever met, which is saying a lot.

All my life I've lived in DC, a city that thrums with power and influence. My best friend's father happens to be the President of the United States. Mine is the Attorney General. If either of our fathers were to find out about tonight at the club or the rules we love breaking all too often, we wouldn't be able to see through the Secret Service agents assigned to keep us out of trouble.

And the only thing standing between us and a massive amount of trouble is Charlotte's bodyguard. The very one who's whisked her away to talk, leaving me here alone with this man who's looking at me like he wants to eat me.

We're tucked into a private sitting area in the back of the club. Demitri sits on the adjacent couch and leans back as a server brings him a glass—a lowball filled with amber liquid.

"Can I get you something?" His accent rolls off his tongue

and skitters across my bare skin, a hot pulse like the one at his neck as he slides his gaze over me.

"I'm fine," I say, though a shot of anything would certainly take the edge off.

The server disappears, and Demitri brings the drink to his lips, taking a small swallow.

"Make yourself comfortable."

I cross my legs and then my arms, the most defensive position I can muster.

He cocks his head a mere centimeter. "I've seen you here before."

"And I've seen you. So what?" My presence couldn't have been that remarkable, but part of me preens a little that he recognizes me.

"What are you frightened of?"

His bold question throws me more than his domineering presence.

"I'm not afraid of anything," I snap.

He doesn't know me. He doesn't know anything about me...

"If you're not afraid, why don't you uncross your arms? I won't bite."

I tense my jaw and contemplate his request. I've just met him, and I've hardly been warm. After a moment, I relent. I exhale a sigh, unfold my arms, and convince myself to lighten up. Charlotte should only be another minute, and then we can get out of here before anyone finds out we sneaked away.

"And your legs."

My jaw falls open at Demitri's last request, which is undeniably laced with sexual innuendo.

I cross my arms tightly again. "I don't think so."

He stares, and my God, it's a look made of blue-eyed steel. Strong, impenetrable, unequivocally dominant. It's all I can do to keep my body's reactions contained, schooled to appear unaffected, when everything he's doing is affecting me. His thumb collecting a stroke of dew on his glass. The deep, rhythmic breathing that ripples the suit that I have no doubt was tailored to accent every obscene muscle in this powerful man's body. But it's his stare that's pulling me apart at the seams.

When I come to the club, I watch, and it thrills me. I'm propositioned, and even the refusal gives me a buzz I've never experienced. But for all the highs I come here for, nothing measures up to this moment under his gaze.

The music transitions to another song and seems to pull his attention away. He turns his head toward the crowded club and the half a dozen scenes playing out. I've lost him.

My heart does something—a half beat, a pause, and then a panicked rush of fast ticks. It hurts. Something about his lack of attention causes physical pain in my chest. So much that I'm uncrossing my arms . . . and my legs.

"Take off your panties." His eyes meet mine again briefly. "No one here cares if you bare yourself to me."

I should tell him to go to hell, but that quickly his attention is somewhere else. Somewhere deep in the crowd, away from me. I bite my lip, hard. I can't believe what I'm doing, but I can't seem to stop myself. I'm trailing my hands up the edges of my dress. Reaching under, I hook my thumbs over the thin straps of my thong and, slowly, drag it down.

Every inch the garment drags down my legs is a prayer . . .

. . . answered when his gaze flickers back to me.

A breath of relief rushes past my lips. Then my panties

are on the floor, dangling off one of my ankles, while my pussy throbs like it never has before.

His eyes hold me there. He's not undressing me. He's undoing me, a tractor beam of intensity right to the heart of me. I can barely breathe.

"You like attention." He lifts his glass to his lips and takes a slow swallow.

I nod. Because, yeah, I like it.

"When it comes from you," I admit, immediately regretting my honesty. This club is wall to wall with Dominants looking to play, and no one else has affected me this way.

A slight squint in his left eye. "Will you entertain me, then? Will you show me something worth watching, kitten?"

Kitten? My whole body heats. Why do I want to purr at this man's feet when he says it? I should be outraged and walk out of here, with or without Charlotte.

But I can't. My knees tremble even as they begin to part. For him. For his steely will that I want to bend to for reasons I can't comprehend.

His tongue takes a seductive sweep across his bottom lip. "*Krásná*," he murmurs.

ACKNOWLEDGMENTS

We of course have to thank Meredith Wild for liking our writing enough to bring us onto the Misadventures team. You've been a friend to us since the beginning, and we're eternally grateful for that.

To Scott, Robyn, and the editing team, thank you for all of your hard work and kind words. You're so great at what you do, and you're a pleasure to work with.

To the rest of the Waterhouse Press team, thank you for your continued support and for designing all of the kick-ass covers and graphics.

The Padded Room, thank you for supporting our craziness. From posting links, teasers, and helping get our name out there, you are a vital part of our dreams. We love you ladies!

To our families, we're not sure how all of you put up with us so we can keep riding along on this journey, but we love you for that and a million other reasons. Thank you :)

MORE MISADVENTURES

Misadventures of a City Girl
Misadventures of a Backup Bride
Misadventures of the First Daughter
Misadventures of a Virgin
Misadventures on the Night Shift
Misadventures of a Good Wife
Misadventures of a Valedictorian
Misadventures of a College Girl
Misadventures with my Roommate
Misadventures with a Rookie
Misadventures with The Boss
Misadventures with a Rock Star
Misadventures with a Speed Demon
Misadventures with a Manny
Misadventures with a Professor
Misadventures on the Rebound
Misadventures with a Country Boy
Misadventures of a Curvy Girl
Misadventures with a Book Boyfriend
Misadventures in a Threesome
Misadventures with My Ex
Misadventures in Blue
Misadventures at City Hall
Misadventures with a Twin
Misadventures with a Time Traveler
Misadventures with a Firefighter
Misadventures in the Cage
Misadventures of a Biker
Misadventures with a Sexpert
Misadventures with a Master

ABOUT THE AUTHORS

Elizabeth Hayley is actually "Elizabeth" and "Hayley," two friends who love reading romance novels to obsessive levels. This mutual love prompted them to put their English degrees to good use by penning their own. The product was *Pieces of Perfect,* their debut novel. They learned a ton about one another through the process, like how they clearly share a brain and have a persistent need to text each other constantly (much to their husbands' chagrin). They live with their husbands and kids in a Philadelphia suburb. Thankfully, their children are still too young to read their books.